What the Island Asks

J. Martin

Island Life Creative Arts, LLC

Chapter One

Arrival

The Bonner Bridge rises out of the marsh like a held breath.

Sera slows without meaning to, foot easing off the accelerator as the road narrows and the water opens on both sides—Pamlico Sound to the west, the Atlantic a presence she can't see yet but feels in the air. The Bonner Bridge, old enough to remember storms it wasn't built for, hums beneath her tires, a low vibration that travels up through the steering wheel and into her hands.

She tightens her grip.

This is the moment she's been skirting since she left Charleston. Not the packing. Not the goodbye calls. This.

Crossing over.

The sky is wide and mercilessly blue, the kind of late-summer clarity that makes everything feel exposed. Heat shimmers above the water, bending the horizon just enough to make distance unreliable. The salt marsh smells green and brackish, alive with decay and insistence. Salt catches at the back of her throat when she breathes in.

She lowers the window anyway.

The air rushes in, thick and damp, threading through the car with practiced familiarity. It presses against her skin, settles in her hair, clings. The island doesn't wait to be invited.

She tells herself it's just a bridge.

Concrete. Steel. Miles logged and crossed by thousands of people who didn't flinch the way she does now. But her pulse has picked up, a shallow rhythm she recognizes too well. Her shoulders creep toward her ears. She forces them down, breath steadying with effort.

This is not the first time she's come back.

It's just the first time she's done it alone.

The water stretches endless and flat beneath her, broken only by grass islands and the dark punctuation of channel markers. A fishing skiff cuts across the sound in the distance, white wake unraveling behind it like a thought she doesn't finish. Pelicans skim low, wings nearly touching the surface, patient and unhurried.

She remembers riding in the backseat as a kid, bare legs stuck to vinyl, her mother's hair whipping loose from its clip as the windows stayed down because the air-conditioning never worked. Her father would hum under his breath, one hand on the wheel, the other tapping time against the door. The bridge felt longer then. Bigger. Like a promise.

Her mother always went quiet here.

Sera hadn't known to notice it at the time—just a shift in posture, the way her gaze fixed on the water as if she were counting something invisible. Years later, memory reframes itself. What once felt like calm reveals itself as distance.

Her father, on the other hand, would point things out. That channel. That sandbar. The way the tide pulls harder on the outgoing, especially near the inlet. He believed in naming things, as if that could keep them from slipping away.

Sera swallows, throat tight.

She's not sure what she believes anymore.

The bridge dips slightly, the highest point behind her now, and Hatteras Island begins to rise ahead—low and long and unmistakable. Houses perch on stilts like watchful egrets. Dunes ripple pale against the darker green of scrub and Loblolly pines. The road curves, inviting and narrow, as if daring her to keep going.

Heat blooms inside the car, the sun pressing through the windshields. She can feel it on her forearms, the familiar weight of it, heavier than Charleston's managed warmth. This heat doesn't pretend to be polite.

She exhales slowly.

The island feels closer than it should. Like it's leaning in.

By the time she reaches the end of the bridge, her chest aches with something that isn't quite fear and isn't quite relief. It's recognition. The kind that doesn't ask permission.

The tires hit solid ground, the subtle shift in texture more felt than seen, and she's here.

No sign. No announcement.

Just the road unfurling ahead, bordered by sea oats bending in the breeze. The wind kicks up suddenly, rattling the car, lifting sand in brief spirals that catch the light before settling back into place. It's as if the island is adjusting itself around her, testing weight and balance.

Welcome back, it seems to say.

She doesn't answer.

She drives on, pulse still elevated, eyes tracking every familiar landmark she pretends not to look for. The old bait shop, repainted but stubbornly crooked. The weathered sign for the turnoff she'll take too soon if she's not careful. The sky so open it feels intrusive.

She's aware, acutely, of who she was the last time she crossed this bridge.

And of who she isn't anymore.

The road curves again, the house still miles away, the past close enough to touch. Sera keeps her hands steady on the wheel and her gaze forward, letting the island have its moment.

It has been waiting.

So has she.

The house announces itself before she reaches it.

Not visually—though the familiar slope of the roof and the way it sits back from the road tugs something loose in her chest—but by smell. Even with the car windows up, even with years between now and the last time she slept here, it finds her. Salt and old wood. Mildew threaded with sun-warmed pine. That faint metallic note of rust and damp that never quite leaves coastal houses, no matter how much you scrub or paint.

She pulls into the drive and cuts the engine.

Silence rushes in, thick and ringing, broken only by the wind moving through the grasses and the distant hush of surf. The house creaks almost immediately, a low, familiar complaint, as if it has been holding itself still and can finally shift again.

Sera sits for a beat longer than necessary, hands resting in her lap, fingers curled loosely as if they've forgotten what to do next. The air feels heavier here. Not oppressive—just weighted with history. With repetition.

She opens the door.

The heat wraps around her, immediate and intimate. It smells like sun-baked cedar and damp shade, like the underside of the house where sand collects and the boards never quite dry. Her shoes crunch softly as she steps onto the gravel, the sound sharp in the quiet.

The front steps sag in the same place they always have.

She knows exactly where to put her foot so it won't creak too loudly, though the knowledge surprises her. Muscle memory rising uninvited. Her hand hovers near the railing, fingers brushing splintered paint worn smooth by decades of palms. The white has yellowed, flaked away in places to reveal older coats beneath, like sediment layers.

The door sticks.

It always has.

She presses her shoulder into it without thinking, the familiar resistance giving way with a muted groan. The sound echoes into the house, swallowed quickly, as if the walls know better than to amplify it.

Inside, the air shifts.

Cooler. Darker. It smells like closed rooms and time. Dust layered over salt. Old paper. A hint of something sweet gone flat—maybe the ghost of sunscreen, maybe just memory filling in blanks.

She pauses on the threshold, letting her eyes adjust.

The house breathes.

That's the only way she can think to describe it. The soft tick of cooling wood. The whisper of air moving through unseen gaps. A loose shutter tapping somewhere down the side, irregular but persistent. The ceiling fan in the living room stirs lazily, blades cutting through the air with a low, rhythmic whir that feels too loud and too comforting all at once.

Everything is where it was.

Not exactly—there are fewer things now, fewer personal touches—but the shape of the rooms remains unchanged. The couch still sags in the middle. The coffee table bears the same water rings, pale circles overlapping like years of neglect mapped in wood. The walls hold their familiar scuffs, the places where furniture bumped and was never moved back quite right.

Sera steps inside and closes the door behind her.

The sound lands with finality.

Her footsteps are cautious at first, soft on the worn planks, as if she's afraid the house might startle. Each board has its own voice. She knows which ones will complain, which will stay quiet. The floor dips slightly near the hallway, the subtle slope something her body compensates for automatically.

She runs her fingers along the back of a chair, dust clinging to her skin. The texture is rougher than she remembers, the finish dulled by years of sun and salt. She rubs her thumb and forefinger together, feeling the grit.

Decay is everywhere if you look closely.

Rust blooming along the hinges. A faint water stain spreading like a bruise on the ceiling near the window. The smell of damp tucked into corners where light doesn't reach. But it's the familiar kind of decay—the expected kind. Nothing sudden or catastrophic. Just time doing what time does.

The kitchen holds the strongest pull.

She steps into it and the scent shifts again: old coffee grounds, the mineral tang of well water, something faintly scorched that might be memory more than reality. The counter bears a shallow nick near the sink, the result of a dropped knife years ago. She remembers the sharp intake of her mother's breath, the way her father waved it off, laughing.

The refrigerator hums steadily, a low mechanical presence that feels absurdly reassuring. She presses her palm against it, feeling the vibration, grounding herself in something solid and real.

This place raised her.

Not gently. Not easily. But thoroughly.

She can almost hear the echo of voices—the rise and fall of conversation, laughter carried from room to room, arguments muffled behind closed doors. The house holds sound the way it holds heat, releasing it slowly, selectively.

Sera moves down the hallway, fingertips grazing doorframes worn smooth by passing bodies. Her bedroom door stands open. The room is smaller than she remembers, the ceiling lower. Light filters in through the thin curtains, illuminating dust motes that drift lazily, suspended.

She breathes in.

The scent here is different. More personal. A trace of something floral long since gone stale. Old books. Linen dried too many times in the sun. Her chest tightens unexpectedly.

This house knows her.

It remembers her weight on the stairs, her footsteps in the night, the way she learned to leave quietly. It has been waiting in its own way, settling and shifting, making space without changing shape.

Outside, the wind picks up, rattling the windows gently. The house answers with another creak, a settling sound deep in its frame.

Sera stands still in the middle of the room, listening.

Nothing resolves.

But everything recognizes her.

The memory comes the way it always does—sideways.

Not as a full scene, not with edges she can control, but as a sensation that slides under her ribs and settles there. The house has shifted something loose. A hinge undone. A door opening without asking.

She stands in the hallway and is suddenly eight years old again, barefoot, the floor cool beneath her feet. The sound of the ocean is louder then, or maybe she was smaller, closer to the ground. She remembers pressing her ear to the wall at night, convinced she could hear the tide breathing if she listened hard enough.

Her mother used to wake early.

Earlier than necessary, earlier than anyone else. Sera would hear the soft clink of a mug against the counter, the measured movements meant not to wake the house. She sees her mother now in flashes—the slope of her shoulders as she leaned against the sink, the way she stared out the kitchen window without really seeing the water beyond it.

There was always water in her line of sight.

Sera hadn't understood that at the time. She thought it was habit. Preference. Only later did she recognize the vigilance in it, the way her mother tracked the tide as if it were a mood that might turn without warning.

Some mornings, her mother would hum. Quietly. Tunelessly. The sound threaded with fatigue. On those days, she would touch Sera's hair in passing, fingers warm and lingering, as if memorizing texture.

On other mornings, she was already gone—out on the deck, standing barefoot despite the chill, robe pulled tight, eyes fixed on the horizon. Those mornings felt brittle. Unreliable.

Her father was different.

Her father belonged to the house the way driftwood belongs to the shore—tossed there, shaped by impact, refusing to leave. He moved through the rooms with confidence, calling out greetings to no one in particular, voice filling space as if daring it to collapse.

He smelled like salt and gasoline and sun.

He taught Sera how to read the water before he taught her how to swim. How to tell if the tide was running fast by the way foam pulled sideways along the shore. How to listen for weather in the wind, the pitch shifting before the sky changed its mind. How to tell how the weather was affected by the never ending clash of the Labrador and Gulf Stream currents.

"This place'll teach you," he used to say, palm pressed flat against the railing, as if the island itself were something solid enough to lean on. "If you let it."

She remembers sitting on the steps with him one evening, the wood still warm beneath them, sky bruising purple and gold. Her mother stood inside the screen door, watching. Not smiling. Not frowning. Just there, hands folded loosely in front of her, as if deciding whether to step out or stay in.

Sera remembers the moment her father reached for her mother's hand.

And the way her mother hesitated.

It was barely a pause. A breath's worth of time. But even then, Sera felt it—something unsteady, something withheld. The island didn't soften that distance. If anything, it made it sharper, clearer, the contrast impossible to ignore.

Her parents loved each other. Of that she's certain.

But they wanted different things from this place.

Her father believed the island could hold them. That it could root them, give shape to a life that made sense. Her mother treated it like a season—beautiful, necessary, temporary. She never said that aloud. She didn't have to.

Sera learned early how to read absence.

The way her mother's voice went flat when talk turned to staying. The way she packed with precision, even for short trips. The way she kept her shoes by the door.

There are other memories, too. Lighter ones.

Running down the beach with the wind tearing laughter out of her throat. Her father lifting her onto his shoulders so she could see over the dunes. Her mother spreading towels, methodical and careful, sunscreen slick and cold against Sera's back.

The island was generous then.

Or maybe Sera was.

She remembers the night storms best. The way the house shuddered under the force of wind, how her mother would sit on the edge of the bed and press a hand to Sera's chest, feeling for calm. Her father would move through the house checking windows, voice steady, confident. Nothing to worry about, he'd say. The island knows how to take care of itself.

Sera knows now that wasn't entirely true.

The island takes what it wants and keeps what stays just like the 5,000 ships that have rested on the bottom of the treacherous coast.

It keeps what stays.

She opens her eyes and the hallway is empty again. The present presses back in, solid and unyielding. The hum of the refrigerator. The creak of the house settling into afternoon heat.

Her parents are gone—one by choice, one by circumstance—and the house remains, bearing the imprint of both. Their differences etched into its bones.

Sera rests her hand against the wall, feeling the faint vibration of wind traveling through wood. The island holds her there, between then and now, memory and breath.

She doesn't know yet what it's asking of her.

Only that it remembers.

And that she does, too.

She senses him before she sees him.

A shift in the air. The way the porch boards answer weight. The house has always announced arrivals—creaks calibrated by familiarity—and her body reacts before her mind catches up. Her shoulders draw back. Breath shallow. The old instinct to brace.

She turns, slowly.

Beckett stands just outside the screen door, half-framed by it, like the house hasn't decided yet whether to let him in or keep him out. One hand rests on the railing, fingers curled loose but certain, the way someone stands when they've learned the ground beneath them will hold.

He's taller than she remembers. Or maybe straighter. Time has put definition where there used to be lean uncertainty. His shoulders fill the doorway easily, not broad in a way that calls attention to itself, but worked-in, shaped by repetition rather than intention.

He's barefoot.

The detail lands with unexpected force. His feet are bare against the weathered boards, skin browned unevenly by sun, veins visible across the top. It's such a Beckett thing—shoes forgotten, unnecessary, an afterthought. The sight steadies her and unravels her in equal measure.

That mommucked look, his jeans are worn thin at the knees, salt-faded, familiar in the way old habits are. The gray T-shirt clings slightly at his chest and shoulders, darkened at the collar with sweat. There's a faint smear of something—grease, maybe—near the hem, like he wiped his hands without thinking.

He looks like someone who has been using his body for work.

Not performing strength. Depending on it.

Her gaze moves without permission. Forearms first—corded, sunburned, scarred in small, unremarkable ways. A pale line near his wrist she doesn't remember, which means it's new. Or newer than she is. His hands are larger than she recalls, fingers nicked and roughened, nails kept short not for neatness but necessity.

She thinks, absurdly, of how careful those hands used to be with her.

His hair is longer now, curling slightly at the ends where salt and humidity have had their way. Darker, too, or maybe the light has shifted. It falls across his forehead in a way that suggests he hasn't bothered to tame it. The island has always rewarded that kind of neglect.

His face—

That's where time has left its mark most clearly.

Not in damage. In decision.

The angles are sharper, the lines at the corners of his eyes etched deeper, earned. His jaw carries a quiet firmness that wasn't there before, as if he's learned the difference between holding ground and digging in.

His mouth is set neutral, but she knows it well enough to read the restraint in it. He's holding something back. Not anger. Not surprise.

Recognition.

His gaze is already on her.

It doesn't roam. It doesn't flicker. It settles.

There's no rush in it, no hunger made obvious. Just attention. Full and unguarded, the kind that takes in detail whether invited or not. She feels it move over her—the fall of her dress, the way the humidity has coaxed loose strands from her hair, the tension she hasn't quite disguised in her posture.

She becomes aware of her hands. One fisted loosely at her side. The other braced against the doorframe, as if she needs the support.

He hasn't spoken.

Neither has she.

The moment stretches—not awkward exactly, but dense. Weighted. Like a held breath shared between two people who know what comes after exhale.

The wind lifts, sudden and insistent, pushing heat and salt air between them. It carries his scent to her—clean sweat, sun-warmed skin, the sharp mineral tang of the sound. Something darker underneath. Cedar, maybe. Oil. A life built close to the water.

Her chest tightens.

This is worse than she imagined.

She thought seeing him would hurt. Or undo her. Or ignite something sharp and immediate.

Instead, it settles into her slowly, the way weather does when it decides to stay.

He looks like someone who belongs here.

The realization lands with a quiet finality.

Not someone passing through. Not someone waiting for something better. Someone shaped by tides and repetition, by the kind of days that end in exhaustion rather than escape.

She thinks of herself then—of the versions of her that left, that learned to hold eye contact in boardrooms, to keep her voice even, her hands still. Of the way she learned to translate herself into something portable.

Standing here, under his steady gaze, that version feels thin. Provisional.

Beckett shifts his weight slightly, the movement subtle but deliberate. The porch answers with a low creak. His fingers flex once against the railing, then still. It's a small thing, but she catches it—the restraint in it, the choice not to move closer yet.

As if he's waiting for her to decide what distance she can bear.

His eyes flick briefly to the suitcase by the door.

Back to her face.

Something unreadable passes through his expression—not judgment, not relief. Just confirmation.

She wonders what he sees when he looks at her. The girl who left? The woman who came back? The gap between those things?

The island exhales around them. Wind through sea oats. The hush of water shifting along the shore. Heat pressing down like a hand at the back of her neck.

Beckett straightens slightly, breath drawn in as if preparing to speak.

And in that fraction of a second—before sound, before language—Sera understands something with quiet clarity.

Whatever they were to each other once is still here.

Not resolved. Not softened. Not gone.

Just waiting to be named.

The pause stretches.

Not the empty kind. Not the kind that begs to be filled. It settles between them with weight, like a held tide, both of them aware that whatever comes next will set something in motion neither can easily stop.

Beckett opens his mouth.

Stops.

Closes it again, jaw shifting slightly, as if he's rerouted a thought mid-sentence. The movement is small but deliberate, and Sera feels it register somewhere low in her chest. He's choosing words. Or choosing not to choose them yet.

"You—" he begins, then lets the sound trail off.

She almost laughs. Almost says it's okay, though she isn't sure what she'd be forgiving. The urge rises and falls, unacted upon. She's learned, somewhere along the way, that rushing to smooth discomfort only hides it. It doesn't dissolve it.

Instead, she shifts her weight, the floorboard answering with a soft complaint. Her fingers loosen from the doorframe, then curl again, uncertain. She's acutely aware of her breathing—too shallow, then too deep—as if her body hasn't decided what rhythm fits this moment.

"Long drive," she offers finally.

It's a nothing sentence. A placeholder. She hates herself a little for it.

Beckett nods once, relief flickering briefly across his face before it's masked again. "Bonner Bridge'll do that," he says. "Makes you feel like you're crossing into something instead of just arriving."

"Yes," she says too quickly, then reins herself in. "It always did."

Another pause.

The wind pushes at the screen door, rattling it softly. The sound seems to give him permission to move. He steps just inside the threshold, careful not to close the door behind him, as if he's leaving himself an exit. Or giving her one.

His eyes move to the house interior now—the walls, the windows, the furniture she hasn't bothered to change yet. He takes it in with the same quiet attention he gave her, and something tightens in her throat.

"Smells the same," he says.

She nods. "I think the house refuses to learn anything new."

A corner of his mouth lifts. Not quite a smile. More like recognition.

"That tracks."

The humor lands softly, then dissipates. Neither of them leans into it. It feels too fragile to press.

He shifts again, hands sliding into his pockets, thumbs hooking on the seams of his jeans. The gesture is casual, but she notices how it changes the line of his shoulders, how it gives him something to do with his hands.

She wonders if he's aware she's cataloging these things.

She almost asks how long he's been back. Almost asks if he ever left at all. The questions line up in her mind like shells along the shore—each one sharp enough to cut if handled wrong.

Instead, she says, "I wasn't sure if you'd still be—"

Here.

Waiting.

The island.

She doesn't finish.

He fills the silence with a quiet exhale. "Yeah," he says. "I figured."

The words are neutral, but there's an undercurrent there—acceptance edged with something else. She can't tell if it's disappointment or self-protection.

She wants to explain herself. To say *I didn't know how to come back before now* or *I didn't think I was allowed to want this anymore.* The explanations stack up, eager and unhelpful.

She swallows them all.

He glances at her suitcase again, then deliberately looks away, as if denying it the power to define the moment.

"How long you staying?" he asks.

The question lands heavier than intended. She feels it in her sternum, the way it presses inward.

"I don't know yet," she says honestly.

His nod is slower this time. Measured. "Okay."

Not good. Not that's fine. Just okay.

Another silence settles, thicker now, threaded with things unsaid. She becomes aware of the space between them—less than an arm's length, more than intimacy. A distance calibrated by history.

She lifts her hand as if to tuck her hair behind her ear, then stops halfway, letting it fall back to her side. The aborted motion feels emblematic somehow—an instinct interrupted by self-awareness.

Beckett notices. His gaze flicks to her hand, then back to her face. Something shifts in his eyes—softens, maybe. Or sharpens.

"Well," he says, clearing his throat gently, "I should let you get settled."

He doesn't move.

Neither does she.

The house creaks around them, the sound old and patient. Outside, the wind slides through the sea oats, carrying salt and heat and the faint metallic note of the tide turning.

This—this suspended moment—is worse than confrontation would be.

Because it means they're both still careful.

Still capable of hurting each other.

Beckett takes a half-step back, creating space without retreating fully. It's a compromise, and she recognizes it for what it is.

"Welcome back, Sera," he says quietly.

Not home.

Just back.

She meets his gaze, holds it longer than comfort would suggest.

"Thank you," she replies.

And in the space between those two simple sentences, everything they haven't said continues to live—unresolved, unspoken, unmistakably present.

She notices the difference in herself the way you notice a scar you've stopped touching—by accident, by reflection.

The girl who left this island believed departure was an act of bravery. She thought movement meant agency, that distance would flatten desire into something manageable. She packed light then. Left things behind on purpose. Treated longing like excess weight.

That girl believed reinvention was a kind of erasure.

Sera knows better now.

She has learned how easy it is to build a life that looks convincing from the outside. She learned how to choose apartments with good light and neutral walls, how to collect furniture that suggests permanence without committing to it. She learned how to introduce herself without mentioning where she came from, how to answer questions with practiced efficiency.

What she didn't learn was how to stop measuring rooms by how quickly she could leave them.

Standing here, in this house that never pretended to be anything else, she feels the contrast sharpen. The island has a way of stripping pretense. Salt air corrodes polish. Weather tests what's real.

The girl she was knows this place by instinct. Knows how the heat settles into bones by midday, how the sound changes color depending on tide. That girl didn't think about belonging. She assumed it.

The woman she became learned to question it.

She learned to translate herself. To make her edges quieter. To turn intensity into competence, desire into discipline. She learned how to be impressive instead of present.

She wonders when that trade happened—when survival began to look so much like success.

Her hands feel unfamiliar to her now. Softer, maybe. Less marked. She notices the absence of small island scars—the rope burn that used to live across her palm, the faint cut on her knuckle from a dock cleat she misjudged once. The body she carries now belongs to rooms with climate control, to schedules that don't bend for weather.

And yet.

The moment Beckett stands in front of her, all of that feels provisional.

She remembers the version of herself that spoke without rehearsing. That stood barefoot on splintered decks and didn't worry about appearances. That believed love could be built the same way boats were—by hand, imperfect, but seaworthy if you respected the water.

She feels older now. Not in years, but in layers. In defenses accumulated and carried without noticing the weight.

She is more careful.

More capable.

Less certain.

Beckett watches her with an attentiveness that makes her feel seen in both directions—past and present overlapping in his gaze. He knew her before she learned how to become someone else. That knowledge sits between them, quiet but undeniable.

She wonders what he sees.

The woman who came back with better posture and worse sleep. The one who knows how to negotiate and compromise and still walks away lonely. The one who learned how to leave before being left.

She wonders if he notices how she still stands like she's bracing for wind.

The island notices.

It presses heat against her skin, lifts her hair with familiar insistence, reminds her—gently, relentlessly—of who she was when she didn't guard every impulse. When she let herself be shaped by place instead of resisting it.

This place doesn't care who she became.

It only responds to who she is now.

She exhales slowly, feeling the truth of that settle somewhere behind her ribs. She hasn't lost herself. She hasn't outgrown this place.

She's just learned how much it costs to pretend you don't belong to what made you.

And standing here, caught between memory and breath, she realizes the most dangerous difference of all:

She no longer knows which version of herself she's willing to defend.

The island answers before she finishes thinking the question.

Wind moves first—not a gust, not the sharp slap of weather turning, but a deliberate push, warm and salt-heavy, threading through the open windows as if the house has exhaled. It lifts the loose papers on the counter, nudges the curtain into motion, finds the hollow at her throat and rests there.

Sera stills.

The heat thickens in response, the way it always does in late afternoon, wrapping her skin in something close to touch. Sweat beads lightly at her spine. The air presses instead of passing through, intimate and insistent. The island does this when it recognizes you. It doesn't rush. It settles.

Outside, the sound shifts. She hears it without looking—knows the water has begun to move again, tide turning with a slow inevitability. The slack has ended. Current slips into the marsh, quiet but determined, pulling at grass and memory alike.

This place never greets you loudly.

It greets you thoroughly.

The floorboards hum faintly beneath her feet as the house adjusts, wood responding to pressure and warmth. Somewhere down the road, a screen door bangs once, twice, the echo traveling farther than it should. A gull cries overhead, the sound sharp and sudden, then gone.

Sera closes her eyes.

She feels the island register her weight. The way it always has.

Not as intrusion.

As return.

The wind finds her hair again, tangling it around her face with casual familiarity. She doesn't brush it away this time. Lets it happen. Lets the heat gather, lets the sound move closer, lets the moment thicken until it feels almost deliberate.

The island has never asked permission.

It has never explained itself.

It only responds—to storms, to absence, to those who leave and those who come back altered. It keeps its own ledger, written in erosion and growth, in what stays standing and what does not.

Sera feels something in her chest loosen and tighten all at once.

The island doesn't judge her for leaving.

It doesn't congratulate her for returning.

It simply acknowledges her presence, the way water acknowledges a body entering it—by reshaping itself around the intrusion, by making space and pressure in equal measure.

Beckett shifts beside her, and the island seems to note that too. The wind changes direction. The air moves between them, threading the narrow space with salt and heat, carrying something unspoken.

Sera opens her eyes.

The horizon beyond the marsh wavers slightly, the line between water and sky softened by humidity. Everything looks close. Immediate. Alive.

She realizes then that this place has been waiting—not in stillness, but in motion. Tides running whether she watched or not. Wind learning new paths around absence. Wood aging. Sand rearranging itself grain by grain.

The island didn't pause for her.

It prepared.

She draws a slow breath, feeling it fill her lungs with salt and memory, and understands with sudden clarity that whatever she thought she was returning to is already gone.

What remains is this:

A place that knows her well enough to change in response.

A place that does not let you pass through untouched.

And standing here, heat pressed to her skin, tide moving again at her back, Sera knows the island has accepted her return—

Without offering any promises about what it will cost.

Chapter Two

The Storm

The storm begins long before the rain.

Sera knows the signs the way you know an ache before weather changes. The air goes slack first, heavy enough to feel held. Cicadas cut off mid-song. Even the sound is slickcalm, its surface smoothed until the water looks like metal in the dark.

She lies awake on top of the covers, the sheet twisted at her calves, listening to the house take inventory of itself.

The tin roof clicks as it cools—small, precise sounds like knuckles tapping wood. A shutter lifts and settles again, testing its hinge. Somewhere in the walls, old wiring hums, steady and patient, alive in a way that makes her think of veins.

She keeps her eyes open.

Insomnia has taught her this habit: vigilance as protection. If she watches the dark, it can't surprise her. She measures her breath. Counts the seconds between sounds. Notes what has changed since the last time she slept here—how the house has aged, how she has.

Heat presses into the room, intimate and unrelenting. Damp wood, salt, the faint metallic promise of rain. Locals used to say storms could smell you, could turn if you weren't paying attention.

Thunder rolls low over the sound. Not a crack. A gathering.

She sits up and swings her feet to the floor. The boards are warm, almost soft beneath her weight. The house answers her movement with a creak that feels less like complaint than acknowledgment.

In the kitchen, she pours a glass of water she doesn't drink. The counter is cool beneath her palms. Outside, heat lightning flickers over the marsh, turning grasses into sharp silhouettes. The storm is pacing itself.

She doesn't startle when she senses him.

The porch boards answer a step. The pause before the screen door shifts. Beckett has always understood thresholds—where to stop, when to wait.

"You okay?" he asks from the doorway.

His voice is careful. He doesn't step inside.

"Storm's loud," she says.

"They get louder when you pretend not to hear them."

Thunder answers him, closer now. The glass rattles. She flinches, surprised by it.

Without thinking, she steps closer.

He notices. Doesn't move.

"You don't have to be alone," he says. Not a question. An offering.

"I'm not good at sleeping through things."

Recognition passes across his face. He lifts a hand, stops short.

"Tell me to stop."

She watches his hand. The steadiness of it. Her pulse picks up.

"I won't."

He exhales—slow, controlled. His fingers brush her wrist. Light. Grounding. Enough.

Rain arrives all at once, hammering the roof, wind driving it sideways against the house. The lights flicker, then hold.

He steps closer, close enough to feel the heat of him, the steady rise and fall of his breath. He doesn't rush. Doesn't crowd.

She tilts her face up. He leans down, stopping just short. Foreheads touch.

"This is still you choosing," he murmurs.

"Yes."

The kiss is slow. Deliberate. A careful press that asks and answers at the same time. No urgency. No claiming. Thunder crests overhead, sharp and immediate.

When they part, just barely, his hand rests at her waist—steady, not possessive. Her palms stay flat against his chest, feeling the solid truth of him there.

They stay like that while the storm spends itself—rain easing, thunder rolling farther away, the house settling into familiar creaks.

He steps back first.

Not retreat. Respect.

"Stay," he says softly. "But only if you want to."

"I do."

They don't move closer again. They don't push past what's been agreed.

Outside, the rain thins to a whisper.

Inside, the space they keep matters as much as the closeness they allowed.

Mutual consent.Mutual restraint.

And for the first time all night, Sera lets herself exhale.

Chapter Three

Beckett

Beckett has always trusted his hands more than his thoughts.

They are steadier than his mind. They know what to do. Net. Line. Knot. Cleat. Winch. Each motion learned young, repeated until it settled into muscle and bone. His hands remember even when he doesn't want them to.

This morning they smell faintly of brine and diesel, the way they always do before the sun clears the sound. He scrubs them at the spigot beside the shed, cold well water biting his knuckles, but the scent lingers anyway. Salt gets into everything. It never really leaves.

He flexes his fingers slowly. No stiffness. No tremor.

The scar along his right thumb pulls tight when he bends it too far. Thin now. Pale.

A reminder.

Work teaches you that.

You rush, you bleed.You assume, you lose something you can't replace.

He dries his hands on his jeans and reaches for the coil of rope waiting on the dock. The fibers are rough and familiar, worn smooth in places by years of use. He feeds it through his palms, measuring by feel alone, coiling it neatly.

Order matters. Out here, disorder doesn't just cost time—it costs boats, men, years.

Not because chaos can't be managed—but because it costs more when it is.

His hands move without his attention. That leaves his mind free to wander, which is always the risk.

He grounds himself in the physical. The pull in his shoulders as he lifts the crab pots. The creak of old boards beneath his boots. The skiff rocking gently against the pilings, impatient to be untied.

Hands don't lie.

They hesitate or they don't. They reach or they hold back.

They leave marks that tell the truth later.

He learned that watching his father work nets along the sound—fingers quick and sure even as the rest of him unraveled. Hands capable. Life less so.

You can mend a tear. You can't force what won't stay.

He tightens a knot and checks it once. Enough.

The dock is cool beneath his palms when he braces himself to stand. The boards give slightly, weathered but intact. This dock has outlasted more than a few people. It knows how to bend.

He understands that kind of survival.

When he works, his hands keep him honest. They don't reach for what isn't offered. They don't take shortcuts that fail later.

That rule extends beyond the work.

Especially now.

He remembers—unbidden—the way his hands hovered the night of the storm. Open. Waiting. The restraint burned, deep and steady, like a muscle held too long.

He shakes it off and reaches for the bait bucket. Fish oil slicks his fingers. The smell is sharp, grounding.

Hands can be washed.

Some things can't.

He keeps his tools clean, sharp, exactly where they belong. A misplaced blade is an invitation to damage. He's seen enough accidents to know how small neglect becomes something irreversible.

The same logic applies elsewhere.

Don't chase. Don't trap. Always leave room for no.

That's enough.

The rest is habit.

He finishes securing the gear, lashing everything down against weather that still threatens offshore. The storm passed, but the sound never rests.

Neither does he.

His hands hang at his sides, empty for once. Broad palms. Strong fingers. Evidence of a life built on usefulness.

They've also let go.

Deliberately.

He curls them into loose fists, then releases.

The last time he waited for someone, the island was kind about it.

That's what made it worse.

It was late summer. The air stayed warm after dark. The sound lay flat as glass, reflecting the last bands of light like it meant to keep them.

He remembers the color of the sky—peach fading to bruised violet—and the way the marsh smelled sweet and thick. He'd leaned against the marina rail, splinters catching at the edge of his palm, watching the road.

He told himself he wasn't nervous. Told himself it didn't matter.

The lie was thin.

Sera had said she'd meet him.

Not a promise. Just an assumption, spoken like staying was simple.

He checked his watch too often. The plastic band stuck to his wrist. His weight shifted, unable to settle.

Headlights passed. Each one lifted his pulse, then dropped it again.

He told himself she was packing. Saying goodbye. Doing what she needed before everything changed.

The dock boards creaked as he paced. A buoy bell clanked somewhere on the water.

Everything else stayed quiet.

The island didn't dramatize the moment. It just kept moving—tide sliding in, insects singing, lights blinking on along the shore.

He drank a beer because his hands needed something to hold.

At some point, the road stayed empty.

He walked home in the dark, boots scuffing sand blown across asphalt. The waves kept breaking. The night air cooled sweat on his neck.

By morning, she was gone.

No note. No call.

The absence did the talking.

Now, years later, the memory surfaces the same way—without warning, without explanation.

He stands at the workbench, fingers resting on the edge. The ache settles beneath his ribs.

He learned from that night.

He learned waiting can look like trusting—until it doesn't.

And he learned never to make someone's absence your home.

He doesn't call them rules.

Rules imply choice. What he has are lessons—paid for.

Don't chase.

Chasing doesn't look like chasing when you're inside it. It looks like effort. Like care. Like being the one who shows up first and waits longest.

He won't do it again.

Don't trap.

Trapping looks like protection if you squint. Like holding tight because you're afraid.

He has no interest in being the kind of man who keeps someone by making it harder to leave.

Always leave room for no.

If there isn't room for no, yes doesn't mean much.

He wants a yes that holds in daylight.

He notices her the way you notice a change in wind—before you name it.

Fragments at first.

A silhouette in the kitchen window. The movement of her hand pushing hair off her face. Bare feet on the porch, toes curling against old boards.

He doesn't stare.

He observes.

Sera moves like someone who has learned how to be watched.

It doesn't suit this place.

The island is loud. Honest. It doesn't reward containment.

He sees the tension in her hands—fingers curling into fabric, thumb pressing into her palm. The habit of control.

The night of the storm, when her wrist offered itself—choice, not surrender—he felt it immediately.

He thinks about it too much.

He notices her scent before he's close enough to speak. Clean. Salt threaded through it.

His body remembers what his mind manages.

He watches her touch the house like she's checking for solidity. Doorframe. Banister. Counter edge.

He understands that.

He notices what she doesn't do.

She doesn't fill silence. Doesn't open wounds.

But sometimes something slips. A soft exhale. A pause when she hears the water.

Those moments undo him.

He stands on the dock with a coil of rope, watching her cross the yard carrying a box. The wind tugs at her skirt. She pauses, adjusts her grip, looks out at the sound.

He wants to take the box.

He doesn't.

He tightens his fingers around the rope.

Later, they pass in the hallway. Shoulders nearly brushing.

He flattens himself against the wall and lets her pass.

She murmurs thanks.

In the kitchen, her elbow bumps his wrist.

He withdraws.

At night, he listens to her moving in the next room.
He doesn't get up.
On the beach, she shivers once in the wind.
His hand lifts—
Stops.
"I'm fine," she says.
He nods.
Storms announce themselves.
People don't.
Storms give you something to do.
People leave you with quiet.
He stands by the marina at dusk, watching the water darken.
Calm on the surface. Moving underneath.
Hope behaves the same way.
Fear keeps you sharp. Hope makes you still.
He's learned to trust storms more than people.
Storms don't pretend.
Sera's return feels like a pressure change. Subtle. Persistent.
He knows what's dangerous now isn't wanting.
It's belief.
He lets the truth settle without naming it.
He wants her to stay.
Not for a night. Not for the storm.
Stay in a way that doesn't require bracing.
The wanting is large. He holds it carefully.
He watches the dark water. Breath slows.
He could walk up the drive. Knock. Check the shutters.
He doesn't.
He stays where he is.

Chapter Four

Morning

S eraphina

She wakes before the house does.

Before the gulls begin their arguments over the sound. Before the wind lifts enough to worry the sea oats. Before the light fully commits to morning. It comes to her in increments—awareness surfacing the way tide creeps in, slow enough to pretend it isn't moving until it's already changed the line of things.

Sera lies still, eyes open, listening.

The storm has moved on. What's left is aftermath: a rinsed hush, the air sharpened and rearranged. It smells cooler—salt and wet pine, a faint green thread of marsh grass. Somewhere outside, water drops from the eaves with patient consistency. The house keeps count.

She becomes aware of warmth behind her.

Not heat.

Weight.

Beckett is asleep.

The fact lands gently and then all at once. Her body registers it before her mind catches up—the solid presence at her back, the slow rise and fall of his breath, the way his arm rests along the edge of the mattress without claiming her, as if even in sleep he's practicing space.

She doesn't move.

Morning has always been the dangerous part. On the island, daylight doesn't rush—it reveals.

Night forgives. Darkness makes room for decisions that don't have to answer for themselves yet. Morning brings clarity. Exposure. The quiet reckoning of what remains when weather breaks and the world returns to its edges.

She's been running from mornings most of her life.

Not always physically—she's stayed plenty of nights, out of politeness or convenience or the simple logistics of distance—but emotionally. Mornings are when she retreats. Mornings are when she begins, automatically, to build a version of the night that can be boxed and labeled: temporary, unrepeatable, safe because it won't be asked to mean anything.

She studies Beckett the way she studies a shoreline after a storm—looking for damage, for signs of erosion, for proof something shifted while she wasn't watching.

His face is relaxed in sleep, stripped of the careful control she's already learned to recognize. The lines at the corners of his eyes soften. His mouth, usually set with intention, slackens just slightly. A faint crease marks the bridge of his nose where the sun has had years to leave its signature.

He looks unguarded.

That unsettles her more than she expects.

She notices details she didn't allow herself to see last night. The way his scarred knuckles rest against the sheet, fingers curled loose as if even rest is something he's had to learn to allow himself. The steady rhythm of his breathing—slow, deep, practiced—like someone who knows how to sleep because he's learned how to wake up alone.

A tightness gathers behind her ribs.

This is the moment when she inventories her exits.

Charleston rises in her mind with the speed of reflex: the clean lines of her apartment, the predictable hum of mornings there. Coffee made in silence. Email before sunlight. A life arranged to keep surprise at bay. She built it carefully, brick by brick, after she left this island with more hunger than certainty.

Here, the morning is too honest.

Light slips through the curtains in pale bands, catching on a worn dresser, a chair draped with clothes she didn't plan to leave there. Dust motes drift lazily, visible now that the air has settled. Nothing is hidden. Nothing is curated.

She shifts her weight slightly, testing reality.

Beckett stirs but doesn't wake, his arm tightening by instinct—just a fraction—before loosening again. The motion is small, unconscious, and it lands in her like a quiet claim of the simplest kind: you're here.

Not desire.

Presence.

She exhales, careful, as if breath itself could tip the balance.

Watching him like this makes something inside her ache—not with wanting, but with recognition. This is who he is when he isn't bracing. When he isn't waiting. When he isn't holding himself in check for her sake.

The thought lands sharp and unwelcome: What happens when he wakes?

Daylight doesn't allow half-truths. It asks for accounting, even if only in small ways: a look held too long, a word chosen carefully, the decision to stay in bed or be the first to leave it.

She's afraid of what she'll see in his eyes.

Afraid it will be expectation.

Afraid it won't.

She slides her hand out from beneath the sheet and rests her palm on the mattress between them, grounding herself in old cotton and solid wood. The house creaks softly, as if acknowledging her movement. The sound is familiar enough to steady her.

She doesn't want to disappear again.

The truth arrives without drama. It surprises her with its plainness. Leaving has always felt easier than staying once morning comes—easier than explaining, easier than risking disappointment. But this morning doesn't feel like a cliff. It feels like standing at the edge of the sound, watching the water decide what it will do.

She turns her head slightly, just enough to look at him one more time.

He hasn't moved. His breath remains even. The moment holds itself open with nothing but her attention.

She lets herself imagine—not promises, not futures—something smaller. Coffee in the kitchen. The sound of his bare feet on wood. Conversation that doesn't hurry to define itself.

For now.

She eases herself up, slow and careful, disentangling without waking him. The floor is cool beneath her feet. She stands, steadying herself, then looks back at the bed once more.

He sleeps on, untroubled.

Sera turns toward the kitchen, carrying the quiet with her, choosing—just for this morning—not to run from what the light reveals.

Morning makes everything visible.

That's what she's always feared—not the light itself, but what it insists on showing. The night can hold ambiguity without judgment. Morning strips things down to their truest shapes. It asks questions simply by existing.

She pauses in the doorway, one hand braced against the frame. The wood is cool beneath her palm. She listens to the house breathe: the slow tick of metal cooling, the faint drip from the eaves where rainwater still hasn't decided it's done.

Behind her, Beckett sleeps.

In front of her, daylight waits.

Fear arrives not as panic but as exposure—a sense of stepping onto open ground with nowhere to hide. She has lived a long time in rooms where she controlled the light, chose what parts of herself were seen and which stayed carefully out of frame.

Morning on Hatteras doesn't allow that kind of curation.

She crosses into the kitchen barefoot, each step deliberate. The floorboards answer in places she remembers. The island makes maps in the body; it doesn't ask permission.

The kitchen smells like rain and old wood and the faint trace of coffee grounds from a life that used to exist here. She opens the window without thinking. Air moves in—salt, marsh, wet sand, something green and alive that feels almost intrusive after years of filtered city air.

She breathes it in anyway.

On the counter sits a shallow bowl of keys she found last night while wandering the house, restless. Her father's boat key. The truck key. A small brass key with its teeth worn down from use. She doesn't touch them. She just registers their presence, as if the house is reminding her what it means to belong to a place: you don't arrive empty-handed. You arrive with history.

She catches sight of her reflection in the dark window glass—hair loose, eyes still shadowed with sleep, the soft vulnerability of a face not yet arranged for anyone. She looks like someone who stayed.

She looks like herself.

The realization tightens her throat.

She reaches for the coffee can, fingers finding the dented lid by habit. The ritual steadies her: grounds measured by feel, water poured into the dented kettle, the click of the burner lighting. These motions belong to her in a way that nothing else does yet. They are small anchors in a morning that wants too much.

The flame catches, blue and sure.

She leans her hips lightly against the counter while the water heats, hands resting flat on the laminate. Her fingers spread without thought, grounding, as if the surface could hold her in place.

Her fear isn't about regret.

It's about meaning.

Night allows closeness to exist without explanation. Morning asks what it's attached to. It turns intimacy into implication. She's learned to avoid that pivot—the moment when desire risks becoming something heavier, something that could demand a choice.

The kettle begins to whisper, then hiss. Outside, the gulls sharpen their voices. The island wakes, unconcerned with her internal calculus.

She thinks of Charleston—not with longing now, but with clarity. The safety of her routines there. The way her mornings were efficient and solitary by design. No witnesses. No one close enough to see her hesitate.

Here, even alone in the kitchen, she feels observed—not by Beckett, but by the house itself. By the memory of who she was here once. By the woman she became when she left.

The kettle whistles—too loud in the hush. She startles, nerves closer to the surface than she wants to admit. She turns it off and pours the water slowly, watching the dark bloom fill the pot. The smell rises rich and grounding.

She pours herself a mug and wraps both hands around it. Heat seeps into her palms, steadying.

This is the moment she usually leaves.

Not physically. Not with suitcases. With distance.

She closes her eyes, mug pressed near her lips without drinking.

What if she doesn't do that this time?

The question is terrifying in its simplicity.

She doesn't have to promise forever to stop running.

She doesn't have to define anything to stay in the room.

She takes a sip. Bitter. Real.

Behind her, there's movement—soft, unhurried. The sound of someone waking without urgency. Her shoulders tense reflexively, then soften as she recognizes the rhythm of it.

She doesn't turn right away.

She lets the fear rise to the surface, lets it hover, waits for it to crest into something that would force motion.

It doesn't.

It lingers, yes—but beneath it is something steadier. A quiet resolve that surprises her with its calm. She doesn't have to flee the meaning. She also doesn't have to nail it down.

Footsteps pause at the threshold.

She feels Beckett's presence before she sees him—the shift in air, the subtle weight of another person sharing the space. He doesn't speak immediately. He doesn't crowd her. The restraint feels intentional, as if he's offering her the dignity of choosing her own pace.

That, more than anything, steadies her.

She turns.

He stands in the doorway with sleep still on him—hair rumpled, jeans sitting low on his hips, his chest bare in the dim light. His gaze moves to her face, not her body, as if he's checking for weather. For strain. For the places she might already be pulling away.

There is no claim in his expression.

No demand.

Only awareness, and something careful held back.

"Morning," he says.

"Morning."

The word holds. It doesn't fracture.

She gestures toward the coffeepot with a small lift of her mug, an offering made without ceremony.

He crosses the kitchen quietly and takes a second mug from the cabinet as if he knows where it belongs. His fingers brush the chipped rim. He doesn't comment. He pours coffee with the kind of attention that suggests this, too, matters.

They don't talk right away.

The quiet isn't uncomfortable. It's precise—like both of them are testing whether the daylight can hold them without forcing them into performance.

Beckett leans against the counter, mug cradled in his palm. His gaze flicks to the open window, the damp porch boards, the clean edge of the morning beyond.

"You sleep?" he asks. Simple. Not loaded.

"A little," she says.

He nods once, accepting the truth without asking for more than she's giving.

She watches him over the rim of her mug. In daylight, he looks more real—less like a memory she can control. The sun makes the faint bruises along his forearm visible, the small nicks that come from work. His thumb traces the mug handle absently, an unconscious motion that tells her he's bracing too.

She sets her mug down before it starts to shake.

"I don't want to pretend last night didn't matter," she says, voice low.

He doesn't hesitate. "Then don't."

Two words. No softness added. No reassurance layered on top. He doesn't offer a promise he hasn't earned. He doesn't ask for one he can't require.

Something in her chest loosens at the clean honesty of it.

She nods once, as if sealing an agreement no one else can hear.

"No promises," she adds quietly. "No pretending I know what comes next."

Beckett's gaze stays steady on her. "I'm not asking for more than what's real."

The words settle between them—solid, fair.

Outside, a gust lifts the damp leaves of the sea grape. Water drops from the eaves and breaks against the porch boards. The island keeps its slow rhythm, indifferent and faithful.

Sera inhales, then exhales, letting the moment exist without trying to capture it.

Nothing has been promised. Nothing has been denied.

For now, that is enough.

She picks up her mug again, and this time her hand is steady.

Presence, she thinks—not as a placeholder, not as an obligation, but as a choice made in daylight, with eyes open.

Beckett shifts closer until their shoulders almost touch. Not a question. Not a claim. Just proximity offered.

Sera doesn't step away.

She lets the space between them close by degrees.

For now, she chooses it.

Chapter Five

Fear

Beckett is already at the docks when Sera reaches the marina.

She doesn't announce herself. She pauses at the edge of the planks, letting the rhythm of the place settle before stepping fully onto them.

The docks are loud in their own quiet way—wood knocking softly against wood, lines creaking under mild tension, halyards tapping masts with irregular insistence. The air smells of diesel, salt, and sun-warmed rope. Somewhere farther down, a gull screams, sharp and impatient.

Beckett stands near the end slip, bent over the open engine hatch of his skiff.

He works slowly. Deliberately. This is not the urgency she remembers from years ago, when everything he touched carried momentum. Now he wipes his hands on a rag before moving on, pauses to listen, adjusts by degrees rather than leaps.

She watches from a distance.

There is a strange intimacy in observing someone who believes himself alone. The way the shoulders settle. The breath evens. Habits surface without performance.

Beckett's hands disappear into the engine housing, knuckles dark with grease. His forearms flex and release with quiet precision. He treats the boat the way her father once did—not as an object, but as something responsive, something that rewards patience.

Memory tugs at her before she can stop it.

Her father at these same docks. Beckett younger then, restless, watching without asking questions. Safety once looked like this: men working with their hands, problems that could be solved if you stayed long enough to understand them.

Beckett straightens, rolls his shoulders once, bends back down. He exhales through his nose—not frustration, concentration.

She realizes he isn't just fixing the boat.

He's grounding himself.

The thought settles heavier than she expects.

His gaze lifts now and then, flicking toward the shoreline, the parking lot, anywhere movement might announce itself. Subtle. Easy to miss.

Waiting.

Not for a part. Not for weather.

For her.

The realization tightens her chest. She hadn't meant to become something he tracked the horizon for.

The dock creaks softly beneath her as she shifts her weight. The sound carries. Beckett looks up.

Their eyes meet.

He stills—not dramatically, just enough to register the change.

"Hey," he says, straightening, wiping his hands again before tucking the rag into his back pocket.

"Hey."

She walks toward him, measured. The closer she gets, the more visible the tension becomes—the slight lift in his shoulders, the way his jaw sets and releases.

"I didn't mean to interrupt."

"You didn't." Too quick. Then quieter. "I was finishing up."

He closes the engine hatch with care, secures the latch, rests his hands on the skiff's edge. For a moment, he doesn't look at her.

She recognizes the impulse.

It's what you do when you need one more second before facing something that matters.

She gives it to him.

"I get strange after mornings like this," he says finally.

She doesn't interrupt.

"I tell myself it's nothing," he continues. "Habit." A pause. "But it isn't."

He looks at her then.

Not desperation. Something folded away too long, opening carefully.

"I keep thinking maybe this time," he says. "Maybe I don't mess it up. Maybe you don't leave."

The words land without force. Unprotected.

Her instinct is to soothe—to promise.

She resists it.

Instead, she steps closer, resting her hand on the edge of the boat beside his. Near, not touching.

"I can't be who I was," she says. "And I won't disappear without speaking."

His throat works. He nods once.

"I don't need guarantees," he says. "I just needed to say it."

Fear spoken, she realizes, doesn't disappear.

But it changes shape.

The wind moves through the marina, rocking boats gently in their slips. Wood knocks against wood. The sound is steady. Enduring.

She stays.

And for now, that is enough.

Chapter Six

The Offer

The letter isn't waiting for her the way people wait.

It doesn't announce itself. It doesn't feel urgent until it's already in her hands.

Sera finds it in her father's study in the late afternoon, when the light has shifted and the house has gone quiet in that specific, coastal way—screens humming faintly, ceiling fan turning slow, the air holding heat but softened by a breeze off the sound. She's been sorting for hours. Papers into piles. Keep, toss, maybe. The mechanics of grief disguised as organization.

The study smells like cedar and dust and old varnish. It's a small room off the hallway with one window that looks toward the marsh, where the grass bends and straightens like it's thinking. Her father's drafting table is still angled toward the light, ruled paper stacked in neat, unfinished columns. A pencil lies exactly where he left it, the tip dulled to a blunt gray.

Sera tells herself she's here for the practical things.

Deeds. Insurance. Bills she doesn't want to open but knows she must. The estate isn't a story. It's a list. Lists are safer.

She slides open the bottom drawer of the old file cabinet, and the metal protests—an exhausted squeal that echoes too loudly in the small space. Inside, folders are packed tight, their tabs handwritten in her father's careful block letters. BOAT. HOUSE. TAX. MISC. She pulls the MISC folder because it's the least specific and, somehow, the most threatening.

The folder is thicker than it should be.

She flips through it slowly—receipts for hardware, a faded registration for a trailer, a stack of old photographs she doesn't allow herself to look at yet. The papers are warm from the day's heat, edges soft from humidity. Her fingertips come away faintly dusty, and she rubs them together absentmindedly, as if she can erase time with friction.

As she looks through the folder she remembers the stack of recent mail she intended to look through.

Not on top. Not tucked away carefully. Just... there, sandwiched between a Charleston business card and an invoice from the electric department. An envelope, cream-colored and too smooth to be an ordinary bill. It looks wrong among the junk mail and bills.

Her name is written across the front.

Seraphina Lockwood.

The ink is dark, deliberate. The handwriting is familiar in the way an old song is familiar—recognizable before you can place it, capable of making your throat tighten before your mind catches up.

Charleston, SC sits in the return address block.

Clean. Typed. Sharp-edged.

For a moment, she doesn't move.

The house makes a small settling sound around her, a muted creak in the beams. Outside, the marsh grass whispers. Somewhere down the road, a dog barks once and then stops, as if corrected.

Sera's thumb rests against the corner of the envelope. The paper is thicker than it needs to be. Corporate stationery. Intention made tangible.

She lifts it carefully, as if it might smear.

The weight of it is almost nothing, and yet her hand instinctively tightens. She has the strange sensation of having been reached for across distance—across years—by a life she thought she had set down neatly, like a file closed and shelved.

She turns the envelope over.

There is no official seal. No red stamp. Just the clean line of adhesive, perfect and unwrinkled. Whoever sent it wanted it to arrive intact.

She looks at her name again. The curl of the S. The slight slant of the letters. She can't decide if the familiarity is comforting or cruel.

It has been years since anyone in Charleston used her full name.

There, she is Sera. Efficient. Polished. Contained.

Seraphina belongs to this island—bare feet, salt-snarled hair, the sound of wind coming through screens at night. Seraphina belongs to her father calling her from the porch when dinner was ready, voice softened by affection he never knew how to show any other way. Seraphina belongs to the parts of her she packed up when she left.

She feels the room tighten around the envelope, as if the air itself has turned slightly denser. The ceiling fan keeps turning, indifferent. The sunlight outside holds steady, gold over green.

She should open it.

She doesn't.

Not yet.

She sets it on the drafting table like it might stain the wood if she holds it too long. It sits there, immaculate, an object too clean for the mess of this place. Her father's pencil lies beside it, humble and worn, the contrast almost insulting.

Sera stares at the envelope as if staring long enough will tell her what's inside.

She doesn't need to know the exact words to understand the shape of them.

An offer, likely. A reminder. A claim.

Charleston doesn't ask. It summons.

She's lived inside that system long enough to recognize the posture of it—business dressed up as opportunity. A door opening that is also a hand at her back.

Outside the study, the rest of the house holds the late afternoon quiet. The sound of Beckett's presence isn't here—no footsteps, no voice—but she feels him anyway, as if the island has wired her senses back into their old channels. She can picture him out on the porch or in the yard, working with his hands, letting time move the way it moves here.

This envelope feels like the opposite of that. Nothing on Hatteras ever moves in straight lines for long.

It feels like a straight line drawn through a place made of curves.

She touches the corner of it again, just once, as if confirming it's real. The paper is cool despite the heat, as though it's brought its own climate with it.

She leaves it on the table.

She closes the file drawer carefully, the metal sliding into place with a soft click that sounds too final.

For the first time since she came back, the island's quiet doesn't feel like shelter.

It feels like a pause before weather.

And on the drafting table, her name waits in ink that doesn't belong to Hatteras, insisting—without a sound—that the life she left might be ready to take her back.

The reaction comes before thought.

Before language. Before meaning.

Sera feels it first in her hands.

A sudden tightening—fingers curling as if the muscles have decided on their own that something needs to be held, or resisted. The tendons along her wrist pull taut, a faint ache blooming where calm had lived seconds earlier. She flexes once, unconsciously, then stills when she realizes she's doing it.

Her breath goes shallow.

Not panicked. Controlled. The kind of breath she learned to take in conference rooms when conversations tilted unexpectedly. In through the nose. Out through the mouth. Minimal. Efficient. As if oxygen itself has become something to ration.

Her stomach drops—not sharply, not dramatically—but with a slow, sinking sensation, like an elevator descending without warning. The floor hasn't disappeared. It's still there. It just feels farther away.

She presses her palm against the edge of the drafting table, grounding herself in the solidness of it. The wood is warm, familiar, nicked and scarred from years of use. Her father's table. A surface built for steady hands and long patience. The contrast makes her throat tighten.

Her body knows this feeling.

It's the same one she used to get when the phone rang too late at night in Charleston. When an email subject line was too carefully neutral. When a meeting invitation arrived without context.

Opportunity wears the same physical shape as threat.

Her shoulders lift without permission, inching toward her ears. She forces them down, rolling them back once, twice, until the tension disperses just enough to be manageable. The ceiling fan hums overhead, its rhythm unchanged. The house doesn't react. It never does.

Her pulse is loud in her ears.

She notices absurd details—dust motes caught in the sunbeam from the window, the faint tick of the wall clock in the hallway, the smell of paper and cedar and old glue. Sensory inventory as defense. If she can name what's around her, she won't have to name what's inside.

She swallows.

The motion is difficult, like her throat has forgotten how to cooperate.

Her body shifts its weight from one foot to the other, a restless sway that feels uncharacteristic here. On the island, movement is usually slow, deliberate. This feels borrowed from somewhere else—somewhere with deadlines and expectations and forward motion that doesn't wait for permission.

Her jaw clenches.

She becomes aware of it only when it starts to ache.

Don't jump ahead, she tells herself. A familiar instruction. One she's practiced until it feels automatic. You don't know what it says yet.

But her body doesn't care about specifics.

It responds to pattern.

Charleston has always announced itself this way—not with urgency, but with inevitability. A subtle tightening. A recalibration. A sense that the ground beneath her has shifted by degrees rather than inches.

She rubs her thumb against the pad of her index finger, feeling the slight roughness left behind by sorting papers all afternoon. The repetitive motion soothes her, just a little. A habit she didn't realize she still carried.

Her heartbeat begins to slow.

Not because the threat has passed, but because her body has moved from shock into readiness.

She straightens, spine aligning with an almost military precision that surprises her. This posture belongs to another version of herself—the one who learned how to sit through difficult conversations without flinching, how to listen without revealing too much, how to hold competing possibilities in suspension.

She hates how easily it returns.

The heat in the room feels different now—less enveloping, more oppressive. She lifts the hem of her shirt slightly, letting air move across her skin. The gesture is small, utilitarian, but it reminds her she's still here. Still in her body. Still on Hatteras Island.

Her gaze drifts to the window without conscious intent.

Outside, the marsh bends in the breeze, green and gold and utterly unconcerned with correspondence or consequence. The sight usually settles her. Right now, it feels like something she's observing through glass.

She inhales deeply this time, deliberately filling her lungs, letting the breath stretch her ribs. The inhale burns faintly, like she hasn't been using her full capacity. She holds it for a count of three, then releases it slowly.

Her hands loosen.

The shaking she hadn't noticed subsides.

What remains is a low, steady alertness—a readiness she recognizes all too well. This is the state she enters when a choice approaches, when something she thought was settled turns provisional again.

She resents the familiarity of it.

Her fingers hover over the envelope on the drafting table without touching it. The space between her skin and the paper feels charged, like static. She can almost feel the future contained inside, folded neatly into corporate language and good intentions.

Her chest tightens again, this time with something closer to grief than fear.

Not grief for what she might lose—but for how easily her body prepares to leave.

She presses her palm flat against her sternum, feeling the steady thump of her heart beneath it. The pressure grounds her, anchors the sensation somewhere physical rather than abstract.

You're here, she tells herself. Right now.

The island answers in its own way—a breeze through the open window, the distant sound of water moving through grass, the quiet insistence of place.

Her body listens.

And for a moment—just a moment—it holds, suspended between instinct and intention, before her mind is finally allowed to catch up.

She doesn't tell him right away.

The decision isn't deliberate at first. It happens in the space between one breath and the next, a small withholding that feels almost involuntary. The letter stays folded where she left it, its presence pressing at the edges of her awareness even as she steps out of the study and into the light of the house.

Beckett is outside.

She can hear him before she sees him—the scrape of wood, the dull thud of something set down carefully, the low, steady sounds of work done without an audience. The screen door opens with its familiar rasp, and heat rushes in, thicker now, late afternoon laying its weight on everything it touches.

He's in the yard, near the skiff pulled up on blocks, shirt sleeves rolled, forearms darkened by sun and effort. He has a piece of sandpaper in his hand, working methodically along the railing he started the day before. Each stroke is even, patient. He isn't rushing. He never does.

She stops just inside the doorway and watches him.

This, she realizes, is what makes the letter feel so disruptive—not what it asks of her, but what it interrupts. The rhythm. The steadiness. The way Beckett exists fully in the present moment, attention given to what's in front of him and nothing else.

He doesn't look up right away. His focus is complete, almost meditative. She watches the muscles in his forearm flex and release, the way his hand adjusts pressure by instinct rather than calculation. There's a calm to it that feels earned, not naive.

Her chest tightens.

She thinks of Charleston—glass buildings, climate-controlled rooms, people who multitask as a form of status. The work there is clean, abstract, rarely leaving marks on the body.

Progress measured in emails sent and decisions made, not in the gradual smoothing of rough wood.

Here, everything shows.

She steps out onto the porch, letting the screen door fall shut behind her. The sound makes him glance up automatically.

"Hey," he says.

"Hey."

He smiles, small and easy, and goes back to his work. The exchange feels normal. Comfortably so. She feels the weight of what she's not saying settle deeper, like something placed gently but firmly on her chest.

She sits on the porch steps, close enough to watch him without interrupting. The wood beneath her is warm, the grain familiar against the backs of her thighs. She folds her hands in her lap, fingers interlacing and unlacing without conscious intent.

He works for another few minutes before setting the sandpaper down and wiping his hands on his jeans. He straightens, stretching his back with a soft grunt.

"You make any progress inside?" he asks.

"Some," she says. It's true, in the narrowest sense. Papers have been sorted. Drawers opened and closed. Nothing resolved.

He nods, accepting the answer without probing. That's always been one of his gifts—knowing when not to ask. She used to love that about him. Right now, it makes her uneasy.

She watches him pick up a hammer, test its weight, then set it aside again. He's moving through familiar motions, muscle memory guiding him. The island has shaped him into someone who knows how to stay with a task, how to let time pass without needing to fill it.

She envies that.

The letter feels like a clock ticking somewhere she can't see.

She studies him closely now, the way one does when they're memorizing something without admitting it. The slight sunburn at the back of his neck. The faint crease between his brows when he concentrates. The way he pauses before lifting something heavy, as if checking himself rather than the object.

This is what she risks losing—not him exactly, but this version of herself that exists near him. The one who breathes more slowly. The one who doesn't feel pulled in multiple directions at once.

She realizes, with a jolt of discomfort, that part of her wants to keep the letter to herself just a little longer. To hold this afternoon intact, unaltered by the knowledge waiting in the other room.

The impulse feels selfish.

It also feels human.

She tells herself she's waiting for the right moment. For the right words. For clarity she doesn't yet have.

In truth, she's watching him, gauging the cost.

He sets the hammer down again and comes to sit beside her on the steps, leaving a careful inch of space between them. The proximity sends a quiet awareness through her—his warmth, the smell of wood dust and sweat, the easy gravity of him.

"You okay?" he asks.

She nods too quickly. Then corrects herself. "Yeah. Just tired."

He studies her face for a moment longer than necessary. She feels exposed under his attention, the way she always has when she's holding something back. He doesn't call her on it. He never does.

Instead, he leans back on his hands, gaze drifting toward the sound. "Storm did more good than damage," he says. "For once."

She follows his gaze. The water lies calm and pale, deceptively gentle. She thinks of how storms reshape coastlines without asking permission, how the most significant changes often happen out of sight.

"Sometimes that's worse," she says quietly.

He glances at her, curious. "Worse how?"

She hesitates. This would be an opening. She could step through it now, let the truth land where it will.

She doesn't.

"Just means you don't see it coming," she says instead.

He considers that, then nods. "Yeah. I guess it does."

They sit in silence for a while, the late afternoon stretching. The island holds them easily, unconcerned with what's being withheld.

Inside her, the tension sharpens—not enough to force action, but enough to make the waiting feel deliberate now. She knows she can't keep this from him for long. She also knows that once she speaks, the shape of the day will change.

For now, she watches him breathe, watches the way his presence steadies the space around him, and understands that withholding isn't about deception.

It's about reluctance to be the one who introduces fracture.

The letter remains unseen.

But its shadow has already begun to stretch across the yard.

The contrast arrives uninvited.

It always does.

Sera notices it in her body before it takes shape in thought—the way her shoulders tense as if preparing for an interior space that requires posture, the way her breath short-ens as though conditioned by ceilings that press rather than shelter. Charleston lives in her muscles, she realizes. In the reflex to be ready. To perform coherence.

She sits on the porch steps and lets her gaze drift toward the sound again, forcing herself to stay where she is. The island holds its shape easily around her. No sharp edges. No hurry. The light falls where it falls, unbothered by schedules or out-comes.

In Charleston, light is managed.

Filtered through glass and blinds and careful angles meant to flatter rooms that exist to impress. The sun there feels decorative, tamed. Even the water—harbor-side and con-tained—moves with restraint, penned in by seawalls and am-bition.

Here, water decides.

The sound stretches wide and unguarded, its surface shift-ing with wind and tide rather than design. There's no pretense of control. No illusion that effort can override weather. The island accepts what comes and adapts without apology.

She feels the difference like a fault line beneath her ribs.

In the city, she learned to curate herself. To sand down edges, to choose clothes that signaled competence rather than comfort. Shoes that required attention. Words that performed clarity even when she felt anything but. She learned how to speak in rooms where interruption was a form of dominance, where stillness could be mistaken for weakness.

She was good at it.

That, more than anything, is what unsettles her now.

On Hatteras, stillness is not absence. It's awareness. Pauses mean listening. Silence is not a void but a field.

She watches Beckett in the yard again, the way he moves through tasks without needing them to mean more than they do. The work is the work. The day is the day. There's no résumé being built here, no future leveraged from present action.

Charleston is all leverage.

Everything is an investment—time, relationships, even rest. The city taught her to think in trajectories, to ask where things were headed before she let herself feel them. She learned to place herself slightly outside her own experiences, narrating rather than inhabiting.

Here, narration dissolves.

The island resists abstraction. It demands presence. Wood splinters if you rush it. Water turns dangerous if you assume it will behave. People notice if you're not paying attention.

She notices, suddenly, how quiet her mind has been these past few days. Not empty—just unburdened by constant re-calculation. She hasn't once checked the time to see if she's late for something. She hasn't scanned a room to assess who holds power.

That absence feels luxurious.

It also feels dangerous.

Charleston represents a version of herself that knows how to survive anywhere. How to land on her feet. How to build a life that functions regardless of weather or attachment. The city doesn't care if you leave. It barely notices when you stay.

The island notices everything.

That is its threat and its promise.

She thinks of her apartment in Charleston—clean lines, cu-rated art, windows that don't open all the way. Climate-con-trolled air humming softly in the background, erasing the need to pay attention to seasons. She remembers the satisfaction of competence, the comfort of predictability.

She also remembers the quiet loneliness of it. The way nights stretched long despite the noise outside. The way intimacy there always felt scheduled, bracketed by obligations.

Here, intimacy leaks into everything. Into the way Beckett stands barefoot in the yard. Into the way the house settles around them. Into the way the island seems to breathe differently when she lets herself match its rhythm.

She realizes the letter—whatever it contains—isn't just asking her to return to a place.

It's asking her to return to a way of being.

The thought tightens something low in her chest.

She doesn't hate the city. That's what makes this harder. Charleston gave her independence. It gave her a version of herself that feels earned. She worked for that life. She built it deliberately, brick by brick.

Leaving it again would not be failure.

But staying here would require something she's never had to give the city.

Commitment without insulation.

She watches a cloud drift across the sun, shadowing the yard briefly before passing on. The light returns, unchanged, unapologetic.

The island doesn't soften its asks.

It offers beauty and demands attention in return. It offers belonging and requires vulnerability as payment.

She understands now why she left the first time. Not because she didn't love this place—but because loving it meant being seen. Fully. Continuously. With no easy exits.

In Charleston, she can disappear into motion.

Here, absence would echo.

She shifts on the steps, the wood warm beneath her palms. Her fingers trace a shallow groove left by time and use. The mark feels honest. Unimproved.

She looks at Beckett again, the way he glances toward her without needing to confirm she's there. The ease of it stirs something tender and unsettling inside her.

Island and city pull at her in opposite directions—not as enemies, but as different truths.

One offers safety through distance.

The other offers meaning through exposure.

She doesn't know yet which cost she's willing to pay.

But for the first time, she recognizes the decision for what it is—not a question of opportunity or obligation, but of how much of herself she's willing to bring with her, wherever she ends up.

The island waits.

So does the city.

And she stands between them, feeling the weight of both, knowing the choosing will change her no matter which way she turns.

She tells him at dusk.

Not because she's ready—she isn't—but because the light has reached that thinning point where the day begins to feel borrowed, and she knows if she lets night arrive without speaking, the silence will turn from pause into omission.

They're in the kitchen.

The windows are open, screens breathing in the sound, and the air smells faintly of brine and something toasted—bread left too long, forgotten in the small rituals of the afternoon. Beckett stands at the counter rinsing his hands, water running steady, unhurried. The sight of him doing something so ordinary almost undoes her.

She leans against the doorway, arms folded not for warmth but containment. She watches the water bead on his skin, the way he shakes his hands once before reaching for the towel. The muscles in his forearms move with a familiarity that feels intimate without trying to be.

She clears her throat.

The sound comes out softer than she expects.

"Hey," she says.

He turns, attention immediate. "Yeah?"

There's no suspicion in his face. No guardedness. Just presence. That makes this harder.

She takes a breath. It doesn't go all the way down.

"There's something I need to tell you," she says.

The phrase lands between them with a quiet finality. Not dramatic. Just definitive.

He stills. Not alarmed. Just attentive in a way that feels almost ceremonial. He sets the towel down carefully, like he's learned not to rush moments that matter.

"Okay," he says.

She appreciates that he doesn't say what. Or are you okay. He gives her space to decide the shape of the truth.

She moves into the kitchen, stopping near the table but not sitting. Sitting would make this feel settled, and nothing about this is. The floor beneath her feet is cool where the sun hasn't reached, grounding in its own way.

"I found a letter," she says.

She watches his face as she speaks, cataloging micro-shifts the way she always has when stakes are high. His jaw tightens—not defensively, just in reflex. His gaze sharpens, then softens again, as if he's reminding himself to stay open.

"From Charleston," she adds.

There it is.

The word hangs between them, heavier than it should be for five syllables. Charleston isn't just a place. It's a direction.

He nods once. Not agreement. Acknowledgment.

"About work?" he asks.

"Yes."

She hates how clean the answer sounds. How manageable. It doesn't begin to capture the way her body reacted, the way the envelope felt like a hinge.

He waits.

The island teaches people how to wait. Beckett is fluent in it.

"They're offering me a partnership," she says finally. "A promotion. A move back. Soon."

She forces herself to keep her voice even. To let the words exist without apology or defense. This is information, not a plea.

Beckett exhales slowly through his nose. The sound is almost imperceptible, but she hears it. Feels it.

"How soon?" he asks.

She hesitates.

It's brief—but it's there. And he sees it.

"I haven't said yes," she says quickly. "I haven't answered at all."

"I didn't ask that," he says gently.

The kindness of it hits her harder than accusation would have. She swallows, throat tight.

"A few weeks," she admits. "They want to move fast."

He nods again. His gaze drifts to the open window, the marsh beyond, the light sliding toward evening. He doesn't look away because he's angry. He looks away because he's thinking.

She feels suddenly exposed, standing there with the truth out in the open and nowhere to put it back. She resists the urge to fill the silence, to soften what she's said with reassurance she doesn't yet believe.

"I didn't want to spring it on you," she says quietly. "I needed to understand what it meant first."

"And now?" he asks.

She meets his eyes. Holds them.

"Now I know I can't understand it without telling you."

That earns her a look she can't quite name—something like respect, threaded with restraint.

He moves closer, stopping a careful distance away. Close enough that she can feel his warmth. Not close enough to touch. The space between them feels intentional.

"Thank you for telling me," he says.

That's it.

No accusation. No assumption. No demand for clarity she doesn't have.

Her chest tightens anyway.

"I don't know what I'm going to do," she says. "I just know pretending this isn't real felt worse than the uncertainty."

He considers that. His hands flex once at his sides, then still.

"I don't want to be something you work around," he says after a moment. Not harsh. Not wounded. Just honest. "And I don't want to make this harder by acting like I get a vote I haven't earned."

The words land with weight.

"I'm not asking you to wait," she says quickly. "Or to—"

"I know," he says, cutting her off gently. "I'm just saying where I stand."

She nods. Relief and sorrow tangle together in her chest.

They stand there, the truth between them like an object neither of them is trying to pick up. Outside, a breeze moves through the screens, stirring the curtains just enough to remind her the island is still here. Still listening.

Nothing is resolved.

But nothing is hidden either.

And that feels like its own kind of turning.

Beckett doesn't move right away.

That's the first thing she notices—how still he becomes, not frozen but deliberate, like someone choosing where to put their weight before stepping onto uncertain ground. The kitchen holds the moment without interference. The fan clicks once overhead. Outside, a skiff idles somewhere down the road, the sound fading as it turns toward the sound.

He takes a breath. Lets it out slowly.

"Okay," he says.

Just that.

No questions stacked behind it. No edge. The word lands level, neither agreement nor dismissal. It feels like a brace more than a response—a way of setting himself before continuing.

Sera waits, heart ticking louder than the clock she can hear faintly from the hallway. She doesn't know what she's bracing for exactly. Anger, maybe. Hurt. Some kind of tightening that would tell her what this costs him.

He turns slightly, resting a hip against the counter. The posture is familiar—casual on the surface, careful underneath.

His hands settle on the edge of the counter, fingers splayed, as if he's grounding himself in the wood.

"They'd be stupid not to offer it," he says after a moment.

The practicality of the statement startles her. She blinks. "You don't—"

"I mean it," he continues, glancing at her. There's no bitterness in his eyes. Just clarity. "You're good at what you do. You always have been."

The acknowledgment hits her harder than flattery would have. He's not minimizing the offer. He's not pretending it's small so he can feel bigger beside it.

She nods once, unsure what to do with the relief blooming in her chest.

He shifts his hands, rubbing his thumb across the counter's edge, a small, repetitive motion. She recognizes it now as something he does when he's thinking—when he's choosing words rather than letting them spill.

"I'm not surprised," he says. "I just didn't expect it to show up this fast."

Neither did she.

He looks toward the window again, gaze settling on the marsh where the light has gone coppery, evening pressing in. The island feels close in moments like this—listening, she's sure of it. He doesn't look away for long.

"I don't need to know what you're going to decide tonight," he says. "Or tomorrow."

She exhales, a breath she didn't realize she'd been holding.

"I appreciate that," she says.

He nods, as if confirming something for himself. "What I need is to understand where we are while you're figuring it out."

The phrasing matters. While. Not if. Not until.

She straightens, attentive. "Okay."

He turns back to her fully now, shoulders squared, expression open in a way that feels intentional. "I'm not going to pretend this doesn't change things," he says. "It does. But I'm also not going to make it the only thing."

The restraint in his voice is almost surgical. He's naming the impact without amplifying it, setting the edges of the truth so it doesn't cut deeper than it has to.

"I don't want you feeling like you have to manage me," he adds. "Or soften it. Or decide faster than you should."

She studies him, searching for the fracture beneath the calm. She finds tension, yes—but it's contained, not denied. Like a rope pulled taut and tied off properly, not fraying.

"That's not easy," she says.

He gives a small, wry smile. "Neither is pretending I don't already know how this usually goes."

The honesty lands quietly, without accusation. He doesn't say you leave. He doesn't have to. The space holds it.

She swallows. "I'm not trying to repeat old patterns."

"I know," he says immediately. "I believe you."

The speed of it surprises her. He doesn't hedge. Doesn't qualify.

He pushes off the counter and takes a step closer, stopping short of her space. The distance remains deliberate, respectful. "What matters to me," he continues, "is that we keep talking. That we don't let this turn into something we both tiptoe around."

She nods. "I can do that."

He watches her for a beat, as if weighing the steadiness of her voice. Satisfied, he nods too.

"I won't make this dramatic," he says. "And I won't disappear into work and pretend that's not what I'm doing. If I need space, I'll say that. If I need time, same."

Her chest tightens—not with fear, but with the gravity of being met this directly.

"Thank you," she says.

He shrugs slightly, the gesture modest. "I'm not doing this for points."

"I know."

They stand there, the truth now integrated into the room rather than hovering over it. The kitchen feels smaller somehow, not cramped but more intimate, as if honesty has closed a distance she hadn't known was there.

Outside, the first cicadas start up, tentative and then louder, a chorus warming into the evening. The sound threads through the open windows, reminding her how close night is.

Beckett glances toward the sound, then back to her. "We'll eat," he says, as if this too needs to be named. "We'll sleep. Tomorrow will still be here."

It's not dismissal. It's care.

She nods again, emotion pressing up behind her eyes. She blinks it back. This isn't the moment for unraveling. This is the moment for staying steady.

He turns toward the stove, reaches for a pan, the normalcy of the movement almost startling. Life continuing. Dinner needing to be made.

Sera watches him, absorbing the quiet strength of his response—the way he's chosen containment over collapse, presence over pressure.

The offer sits between them now, real and unignored.

And for the first time since she found the letter, she understands that leaving is no longer an abstract future.

It's a possibility with weight.

One that has already begun to change the shape of the room.

The shift doesn't announce itself.

It arrives quietly, almost politely, like a tide change you don't notice until the water's already pulling differently around your ankles.

They cook together without touching.

Not pointedly. Not to prove anything. Just the way two people do when the shape of the room has altered and their bodies are adjusting before their minds catch up. Beckett moves with the same ease he always has—opening drawers without looking, setting the pan just so on the burner—but there's a new deliberateness to it, as if he's measuring the edges of himself now.

Sera feels it immediately.

The absence where contact would have been. The space he leaves between their shoulders as they pass each other. The way he hands her the salt instead of brushing past to reach it himself.

Nothing is withheld.

Everything is chosen.

She tells herself she imagined it, that this is what honesty looks like once it's spoken aloud—quieter, less charged. But her body knows better. Desire hasn't gone anywhere. It's simply changed posture.

Dinner is simple. Fish from the sound, vegetables she found in the back of the fridge, bread warmed in the oven. They sit across from each other at the small table, knees not touching this time. Conversation stays light, almost careful—weather, the boat he's working on tomorrow, a neighbor she ran into earlier who asked after her father.

They are practicing.

Not distance. Presence.

She watches his hands as he eats—how he pauses before cutting, how he sets his fork down when he listens. Earlier, those hands had felt like invitation. Now they feel like boundary, and the realization sends an unexpected ache through her chest.

After dinner, he clears the plates without comment. She follows him to the sink, handing him a towel. Their fingers brush, just briefly.

The contact lands sharper than it did before.

They both feel it. They both let it go.

Outside, the light has thinned to that deep blue hour when the island feels suspended between states. Sera steps onto the porch, the boards still warm from the day. Beckett joins her a moment later, carrying two mugs of coffee he didn't ask if she wanted.

He hands her one.

Their fingers don't touch this time.

They sit side by side on the steps, facing the sound. The water has darkened, smooth and reflective, the last light caught like a held breath. A breeze moves through the marsh grass, carrying the faint brackish smell that always makes her think of endings disguised as beginnings.

"This feels different," she says quietly.

He doesn't pretend not to know what she means. "Yeah."

Not regret. Recognition.

"I don't want it to feel like I pulled back," he adds after a moment.

She shakes her head. "You didn't."

"I just..." He trails off, searching. His thumb rubs the rim of his mug, a small grounding motion. "I don't want to lean on something that might be moving."

The care in the words catches her off guard. He isn't protecting himself from her. He's protecting them from a false footing.

"I get that," she says.

And she does. More than she wants to.

The night sounds settle around them—crickets, distant engines, the slap of water against the dock somewhere down the road. The island resumes its steady rhythm, indifferent to the recalibration happening on this porch.

She shifts slightly, close enough that their arms brush. This time, he doesn't move away.

The contact is gentle. Neutral. Weighted with choice.

They sit like that for a while, neither speaking, both aware of how much restraint is living in the space between them. It feels almost intimate in its own way—this mutual decision not to reach for what would be easy.

When he finally stands, he does it slowly, as if giving her time to say something if she needs to. She doesn't.

"I'm going to turn in," he says. "Long day tomorrow."

She nods. "I'll be there in a bit."

He hesitates, then leans down and presses a brief kiss to her temple. It's chaste. Grounded. Full of intent.

"Good night, Sera."

"Good night."

He goes inside, the screen door whispering shut behind him. The sound lingers longer than it should.

She stays on the porch, mug cooling in her hands, watching the sound darken fully. The island feels closer now, not in comfort but in consequence. Everything familiar is suddenly fragile in a way it wasn't before.

She realizes then that intimacy hasn't disappeared.

It's simply become honest.

And honesty, she knows, has weight.

Behind her, the house settles. Ahead of her, the water keeps moving, indifferent and inevitable.

For the first time since she returned, the idea of leaving is no longer hypothetical.

It has entered the room.

And nothing—no matter how carefully held—will be untouched by it.

Chapter Seven

Low Tide

The days don't collapse into each other so much as they thin.

They become a series of small, competent motions—Sera moving through the house with a legal pad, Beckett moving through the yard with tools, both of them circling the same rooms with the careful awareness of people sharing space that has started to mean something.

Mornings begin early now.

The light comes in pale and clean, and the sound is already awake—boats in the distance, gulls starting their arguments, the faint hum of traffic toward Hatteras Village. Sera wakes to the soft press of heat against the screens and the smell of coffee she didn't make.

Beckett is always up before her.

Not pointedly. Not as a statement. It's simply who he is—someone shaped by tide tables and weather windows. She hears him in the kitchen: a cupboard opening, the tap running, the muted clink of a mug against the counter. Then the screen door. Then the quiet of his absence.

When she steps into the kitchen, the mug is left for her by the sink, steam already gone, coffee dark and strong the way he drinks it. The gesture is gentle. Thoughtful.

It doesn't ask for anything.

And somehow that's what makes it ache.

She drinks it standing up, leaning her hip against the counter, eyes on the marsh through the window. Her phone sits face-down beside her notebook, a quiet threat. Most days it doesn't buzz. Some days it does. Either way, she can feel it there, a second horizon.

Her father's study becomes her territory.

She sorts paperwork until the words blur—deed, title, appraisal, account. She learns the language of ending in a way she hasn't had to before. Grief comes in strange forms: the discovery of a receipt for nails, the note her father left in the margin of a boat plan, a repaired hinge that still squeaks because he never got around to fixing it properly.

The house holds all of it without comment.

Beckett works outside.

She sees him through windows, framed by light and movement: shoulders bent over a railing, head lowered over an engine, hands steady at tasks that respond to patience. He disappears for hours—out on the water, out to a job site, out into the kind of life that doesn't pause just because something in him has.

He comes back sunburned and salt-worn, smelling like diesel and wind.

They talk in the evenings.

Not about the letter. Not directly.

They talk about weather, about the neighbor's dog that keeps getting loose, about the grocery truck that only comes certain days to the village. They build small bridges out of ordinary things, as if ordinary is safer.

Sometimes she catches him watching her the way he watched her at the marina—quietly, attentively, as if memorizing details he doesn't want to lose. When she meets his eyes, he doesn't look away.

But he doesn't step closer either.

They move around each other like a tide that refuses to rise.

Shared space without shared intimacy.

They pass in the narrow hallway and their shoulders almost touch. Almost always. The almost becomes its own language: I still want you. I don't know what to do with wanting.

At night, they sleep in the same house, sometimes the same bed, but the heat between them has shifted. It isn't gone. It's simply... held. Contained behind restraint that feels newly deliberate.

Sera lies awake some nights, listening to the house settle and the distant sound of waves beyond the dunes, and thinks about how easy it would be to reach for him in the dark, to let the night blur edges again.

She doesn't.

Not because she doesn't want to.

Because she can feel the shape of what it would become—a borrowed comfort, an argument postponed by skin.

She refuses to let their bodies lie better than their words.

Days pass like that.

Tide charts pinned to the fridge. Sand in the entryway. A growing stack of sorted papers on the dining table. Her father's estate becoming more real by the day in the most mundane ways. The offer from Charleston becoming heavier not because it's mentioned, but because it isn't.

One afternoon, the wind shifts cooler, and the sky takes on that washed-out blue that means weather is changing somewhere farther offshore. Beckett comes in with a sunburned nose and a quiet tiredness around his eyes.

"You wanna walk?" he asks.

It's casual. Almost offhand.

But she hears the carefulness beneath it—the way he offers something that isn't the bed, isn't the kitchen, isn't the charged corners of the house where their silence lives too loudly.

"Yes," she says.

They go to the beach before the light starts to fail.

The sand is cool under her feet, packed firm near the waterline. The tide is low—so low the wet flats stretch wide and glistening, rippled like hammered metal. Tide pools hold trapped pieces of the sound: small fish, sand dollars, the occasional crab scuttling sideways with offended purpose.

The world looks stripped down at low tide.

Honest.

Beckett walks beside her without speaking for a long time. The wind lifts his hair, tugs at his shirt. He looks out toward the inlet like he's reading something in the water she can't see.

Sera listens to their footsteps—the soft press and release of sand underfoot, the hush of water over flats. She feels the distance between them like a third presence.

Finally, she says, "This is your favorite time."

He glances at her. "Low tide?"

"You always used to say you could see what was really there."

He nods once, a quiet acknowledgement of the memory. "You can. If you're willing to look."

They stop near a stretch of exposed sandbar where shells have collected in a white line like evidence. The wind comes clean off the water, cooling the sweat at the back of her neck.

Sera folds her arms loosely, more for steadiness than warmth. "Is that what this is?" she asks before she can talk herself out of it. "Looking?"

Beckett doesn't pretend not to understand.

He watches the water for a beat longer, then looks at her fully. The steadiness in his gaze makes her stomach tighten.

"I think so," he says.

"And what do you see?" she asks, voice quiet.

He exhales slowly. "I see you trying," he says. "And I see you still holding one foot on the other side."

The words aren't sharp.

They don't need to be.

Sera's throat tightens. "I'm not doing it on purpose."

"I know," he says. And then, after a pause, "That's part of what scares me."

The wind pushes at them, tugging the hem of her shirt, lifting sand in faint, whispering sheets. The beach feels vast around them, the low tide making the distance to the water seem farther than it is.

Beckett steps closer—not enough to touch, just enough that she feels the warmth of him despite the wind.

"I'm not asking for a decision today," he says, voice calm. "But I can't—" He stops, breath catching once, then steadies. "I can't be the thing you come back to when it's convenient."

Sera's chest aches, sharp and immediate.

He keeps his gaze on hers. "Temporary," he says, as if tasting the word, "stopped working for me a long time ago."

The sentence lands like a line drawn in sand.

Not as a threat.

As truth.

And Sera realizes, standing on the exposed flats of low tide with the island breathing around them, that he's right.

Temporary—whatever it meant before—has become unacceptable.

They share the house the way people share a shoreline after a storm—aware of every altered contour, every place the water reached and then withdrew.

Nothing is overtly wrong.

That's the strangest part.

Doors still open. Coffee still appears in the morning. Beckett still asks if she's eaten when the day runs long, still leaves a towel draped over the chair on the porch when he comes in from the sound. Sera still folds laundry left too long in the dryer, still sets an extra plate on the table before remembering she doesn't need to.

Their lives continue to overlap in small, competent ways.

But intimacy has shifted its weight.

They move through rooms with an almost uncanny awareness of each other's bodies. Not in hunger—at least not only that—but in calibration. When she enters the kitchen, Beckett adjusts where he's standing without seeming to. When he crosses behind her in the hallway, he keeps a careful inch of space that wasn't there before. Their bodies have learned a new grammar.

At night, the house feels larger.

Sera lies awake listening to the sound of Beckett's footsteps in the other room, the way the floor creaks slightly more under his weight. She knows his patterns now—how he pauses near the window, how he checks the latch on the back door, how he stands still for a beat before turning off the light, as if making sure the quiet has settled properly.

Sometimes he sleeps beside her.

Sometimes he doesn't.

Neither of them comments on it.

When he does, the space between them is deliberate. Their legs don't tangle the way they once did. His arm rests near her shoulder, not over it. The closeness feels held in suspension—intimate without being indulgent.

Sera misses the weight of him.

She misses the easy reach, the way his presence once felt like permission to exhale fully. But she understands what's happening, even if she doesn't know how to fix it. Desire hasn't vanished. It's been disciplined.

And discipline, she's learning, can ache as sharply as denial.

In the mornings, they pass each other quietly.

She'll be at the sink, rinsing a mug, when he comes in smelling like sun and salt. He'll pause just long enough to say her name, soft and neutral, like a touch he's choosing not to take.

She'll answer the same way.

They talk about practical things—groceries, schedules, the weather offshore. They don't talk about what they're avoiding.

The house becomes a map of near-misses.

The back porch where they once sat too close now holds a careful gap between their chairs. The narrow staircase that used to bring them shoulder to shoulder now feels suddenly wide. Even the couch seems to insist on space, cushions settling into a shape that doesn't invite.

Sera notices how Beckett keeps his hands busy.

Always repairing something. Sanding, tightening, cleaning. When he sits, he leans forward, elbows on his knees, hands clasped—not restless, but contained. As if stillness might invite something neither of them is ready to navigate.

She mirrors him without meaning to.

She organizes. Reorganizes. Makes lists she doesn't follow. Moves objects that don't need moving. When she sits, she folds herself in just enough to feel compact, guarded.

They are protecting something.

She just isn't sure what yet.

Once, in the late afternoon, she finds him in her father's study, standing at the window with a boat plan rolled loosely in his hands. He doesn't turn when she enters. He doesn't have to. The room feels aware of both of them.

"I didn't mean to interrupt," she says.

"You didn't," he replies.

She stands in the doorway for a moment, watching the way the light catches the edges of the paper, the careful way his fingers hold it—not gripping, not loose. Respectful.

"My dad used to say you could tell a lot about a person by how they handle things that don't belong to them," she says quietly.

Beckett nods. "He wasn't wrong."

They stand there together, the space between them full of shared history and unsaid want. She wants to step closer. She doesn't.

Neither does he.

Later, she realizes that's the point.

They are choosing not to collapse the distance prematurely. They are letting it exist long enough to be named.

The nights stretch longer.

The island shifts toward that late-summer lull where heat settles in layers and the wind dies down just enough to make everything feel exposed. The quiet presses close, amplifying every small sound—the click of a light switch, the soft thud of a door closing, the sigh of the house settling into itself.

Sera lies awake, staring at the ceiling fan turning slow and steady, and thinks about how intimacy isn't always loud. Sometimes it's this—the careful shaping of absence, the way restraint sharpens awareness.

She feels Beckett's presence even when he isn't beside her. Especially then.

When he passes her in the morning and pauses, just for a fraction of a second too long, like he might say something and then decides against it. When he hands her a glass of water without letting their fingers touch. When he looks at her and then deliberately looks away.

Shared space.

Unshared intimacy.

It's not rejection.

It's something far more fragile.

And Sera knows—deep in the place where the island has always spoken to her—that this careful distance can't hold forever.

They go to the beach when the tide is at its lowest.

Not intentionally—at least not out loud—but Sera knows the signs now. The way the water pulls back farther than it should. The wide, exposed flats shining like hammered tin. The smell shifts too, sharper, more mineral, as if the island has turned itself inside out and left its bones visible.

Low tide always feels like confession.

They park near the access road just south of the village, where the dunes dip enough to let the wind through. The sky is a pale, washed blue, high and cloudless, the kind that makes everything feel unguarded. Sera slips off her sandals and lets the sand take her weight, cool and firm beneath her feet.

Beckett walks a few steps ahead of her, hands in his pockets, shoulders relaxed but not loose. He hasn't looked back yet. She knows better than to read that as distance. It's simply how he moves here—like someone giving the water room to speak first.

The beach is quiet in that particular low-tide way. Not empty, but spread out. Sound carries differently when the water retreats. Every footstep lands more clearly. Every gull call feels closer.

They walk parallel to the waterline, not quite at the edge. The sand here is smooth, marked with ripples and shallow pools that catch the light. Small fish dart in the trapped water, flashes of silver panicking against temporary boundaries.

Sera watches one pool until a wave finally reaches it, collapsing the space and releasing what was held.

She feels it in her chest.

Low tide does this to her—makes her aware of what's been exposed without her permission.

Beckett stops near a stretch of wet sand where shells have gathered in a thin, uneven line. He crouches, picks one up—a spiral whelk, worn smooth by time and water—and turns it over in his hand. The gesture is absentminded, reverent.

"My dad used to bring me here when it looked like this," she says, surprised by the memory as it surfaces. "Said you could tell what kind of season it'd been by what washed up."

Beckett straightens, glances at the shells. "What kind was it?"

She considers. "Hard," she says finally. "But honest."

He nods. Doesn't comment. He understands the language of that kind of truth.

They walk on.

The distance between them stretches and contracts with the terrain. Sometimes the sand narrows and they pass close enough that their arms brush. Sometimes it widens and they drift apart without remark. The movement feels organic, responsive—like they're letting the beach decide the space.

Sera breathes in deeply. The air tastes clean here, stripped of sweetness, all salt and iron and sun-warmed sand. It fills her lungs in a way that feels bracing rather than comforting.

She thinks of Charleston then—not because she wants to, but because the contrast insists on itself. The way the city presses upward, inward. The controlled lines, the curated edges. How water there is something you look at, not something that moves you.

Here, the water dictates.

Beckett slows, letting her catch up. When she does, he gestures toward the flats. "You can see how far it goes out today."

She nods. "It makes everything look farther away than it is."

"Or closer," he says. "Depends on how you're looking."

She studies the horizon—the thin, shimmering line where water meets sky. It feels both distant and immediate, like a decision she's been circling without naming.

They stop near a tidal creek cutting its way back toward the sound, shallow and winding. The water slides through it quietly, persistent, finding its way even in retreat.

"This is when the island shows you what it's made of," Beckett says. "Low tide."

She smiles faintly. "And what are we made of?"

The question slips out before she can stop it.

He doesn't answer right away.

He watches the water instead, eyes narrowed slightly against the glare. When he does speak, his voice is even, thoughtful.

"I think," he says, "we're seeing how much we're willing to leave uncovered."

The words settle between them, heavy and precise.

She feels suddenly bare—not exposed exactly, but visible in a way that demands honesty. Low tide doesn't invent anything. It only reveals.

A breeze moves across the flats, lifting the hem of her shirt, tugging at Beckett's hair. The sun presses warm against her shoulders. Everything feels stripped down to essentials.

She steps closer, close enough that their shadows overlap. He doesn't move away. He doesn't step closer either.

They stand there, the island stretched wide around them, the water pulled back, waiting.

Sera understands then why this place has always undone her.

Because it doesn't let you hide behind fullness.

Because it insists you see what remains when everything else recedes.

And standing at literal low tide, with Beckett beside her and no promise to lean on, she feels the erosion not as loss—but as warning.

What's left will matter more than what was easy.

They walk for a while before either of them speaks.

The beach opens wide again, the flats stretching pale and reflective, the water pulled so far back it feels like an invitation and a dare at once. Sera lets the rhythm of their steps settle—press, release, press—until the sound of it becomes a kind of thinking. Beckett keeps pace beside her, neither leading nor following, the distance between them measured but not cold.

"You ever notice," she says finally, "how people talk about staying like it's passive?"

He glances at her, curious. "Passive how?"

"Like it just happens," she says. "Like you wake up one day and realize you never left."

He nods slowly. "Yeah."

They pass a shallow pool where the water trembles with life—minnows flashing, a crab half-buried, its eye stalks lifted like questions. Beckett pauses to watch it for a second, then straightens.

"Staying takes work," he says. "Leaving does too. People just like to pretend one of them is easier."

Sera considers that. The sun presses against her neck; she can feel heat building there, the slow insistence of it. "In the city," she says, "leaving is framed like ambition. Staying is framed like settling."

"And here?" he asks.

She looks out over the flats. "Here it's the opposite. Staying is loyalty. Leaving is escape."

Beckett exhales through his nose, a sound that's almost a laugh. "Neither one's wrong."

"No," she agrees. "But they both cost something."

They stop near the tidal creek again, the narrow ribbon of water finding its way back toward the sound. Beckett crouches, skims a hand through the current. It's cold enough to make him wince. He shakes his hand once, droplets catching the light before falling back.

"My dad used to say the island doesn't trap you," he says. "It just asks you to be honest about why you're here."

Sera's chest tightens. "What did he say about leaving?"

"That it doesn't save you," Beckett replies. "It just changes the questions."

She nods. The truth of it settles into her bones. She thinks of Charleston—the careful distances, the polished rooms, the way ambition there is both currency and shield. She thinks of the island—the way it keeps score in subtler ways, through weather and waiting and who shows up after storms.

"I used to think leaving meant I was choosing myself," she says quietly.

"And now?"

"And now I'm not sure," she admits. "I think I was choosing certainty. Or the illusion of it."

Beckett straightens, dusts sand from his palms. "Certainty's expensive," he says. "Costs more than people expect."

They start walking again, slower now. The beach feels larger at this hour, the low tide exposing so much ground it's hard to tell where the water will return first. Sera feels the pull of the horizon like a line drawn through her.

"Do you ever wonder," she asks, "if staying too long makes you smaller?"

He thinks about that. She can tell—by the way his gaze shifts, by the pause before he answers. "I think it can," he says. "If you stop choosing it. If you stay because you're afraid to move."

"And leaving?" she presses.

"That can make you smaller too," he says. "If you keep running from the same thing."

She stops walking. He does too, immediately, as if tethered.

"I don't want to be afraid," she says. The admission feels like stepping into cold water—bracing, honest. "Of staying or leaving."

"I know," he says.

The wind moves through the dunes, carrying the faint rattle of sea oats. The sound threads through the quiet, a reminder that nothing here is ever truly still.

"I don't need you to choose this place," Beckett says after a moment. His voice is steady, careful. "Or me. I just need you to know what you're choosing when you do."

She looks at him then—really looks. The lines at the corners of his eyes, the sunburn just beginning to peel along his nose, the way he stands like he's learned not to lean on anything that might move. There's no demand in his expression. No ultimatum.

Just a boundary spoken gently enough that it doesn't bruise.

"What if I don't know yet?" she asks.

"Then you don't know yet," he says. "But we don't pretend that not knowing doesn't matter."

The words land clean and sharp, like air after rain.

They stand there, the island holding its breath around them. The tide is still low, the flats still exposed, but Sera can feel the pull changing—subtle, insistent. The water will return. It always does.

She nods once. "I don't want to make a life out of postponing."

Beckett's mouth curves—not a smile exactly, but something close. "Neither do I."

They start walking again, shoulder to shoulder now, close enough that the warmth of him seeps through the space they've been keeping. The conversation doesn't resolve anything. It isn't meant to.

It names the shape of the choice.

And that feels like the beginning of something that can't be deferred forever.

They stop without deciding to.

The shoreline curves inward here, the flats narrowing into a stretch of damp sand where the water has begun its slow return. The first thin fingers of tide slip across the surface, reclaiming space quietly, as if not to draw attention to themselves. The light has softened, the sun lowering enough to take the edge off the heat without cooling it entirely.

Sera feels it before she names it—that sense of a moment arriving fully formed, asking only whether she'll meet it or step aside.

Beckett turns toward her. Not abruptly. Not with intent that feels rehearsed. He looks at her the way he has been all afternoon—attentive, measured—but something in his expression has shifted. Less guarded. More present.

She realizes then that the distance they've been holding has done its work.

It has clarified rather than erased.

"This feels like one of those days," she says quietly.

He studies her face, searching for context. "What kind?"

"One I'll remember whether I want to or not."

The honesty in the statement surprises them both.

Beckett's gaze drops briefly—to her mouth, maybe, or the line of her jaw—before returning to her eyes. The movement is subtle, restrained. Acknowledged and then contained.

"We don't have to do anything," he says.

She nods. "I know."

The tide advances another inch, water curling around her toes, cool and deliberate. She breathes in deeply, the smell of wet sand and salt filling her lungs. The island feels closer now, the way it does when something is about to change.

She steps toward him.

It's small—just enough to close the remaining space. He doesn't move away. He doesn't step forward either. He lets the choice land squarely with her.

Her hand lifts without urgency, fingers brushing the back of his wrist. The contact is light, exploratory. She feels the warmth there, the pulse beneath skin, the stillness of someone choosing not to rush.

He exhales slowly.

"If this is just a moment," he says softly, "we let it be just that."

The care in his voice nearly breaks her.

"It is," she says. "But that doesn't make it meaningless."

"No," he agrees. "It doesn't."

She leans in, closing the last inch herself.

The kiss is gentle.

Unhurried.

Not the kind that reaches or claims or promises anything beyond its own existence. Their mouths meet with a softness that feels almost reverent, like they're touching something fragile and choosing not to test its limits. The world narrows, not into urgency, but into focus.

She feels his hesitation—present, not resistant. A pause that isn't doubt but respect. She responds by pressing her hand more firmly against his wrist, grounding them both.

That's all it takes.

The kiss deepens slightly, not in heat but in intent. It's layered with recognition, with the quiet understanding that this isn't about what comes next. It's about marking what already exists.

She tastes salt on his lips. Feels the faint scrape of sun-roughened skin against her cheek. The wind moves around them, lifting her hair, threading through the space they occupy as if trying to memorize it too.

He rests his forehead against hers when they part, eyes closed for a brief second longer than necessary.

They don't speak.

They don't need to.

The water reaches higher now, washing over the place where they stood, erasing the impressions of their feet in the sand. Sera watches it happen, aware of the metaphor without feeling trapped by it.

"This isn't a promise," she says quietly, more to name it than to defend it.

"I know," he replies.

"And it's not goodbye."

"I know that too."

They stand there for a moment longer, close enough to feel each other's breath, not close enough to blur the clarity they've earned. When she steps back, it isn't a retreat. It's a choice.

He lets her go without reaching after her.

The restraint feels as intimate as the kiss itself.

They turn and begin walking again, side by side, their shoulders occasionally brushing as the beach narrows further. The tide continues its steady return, reshaping the shore behind them.

Sera carries the kiss with her—not as anticipation, not as leverage, but as memory.

Something real.

Something chosen.

And she knows, with a certainty that settles deep and quiet in her chest, that this moment will not ask more of them than they can give.

Not yet.

They don't say it out loud, but it moves with them all the same.

Time, thinning.

It shows up in the smallest calibrations—in the way Beckett checks his watch more often, not because he's late for anything, but because he's begun counting days without admitting to it. In the way Sera catches herself memorizing ordinary details: the nick in the kitchen table where her father dropped a hammer once, the sound Beckett makes when he laughs under his breath, the exact angle of light on the marsh in late afternoon.

None of it feels urgent.

That's what makes it dangerous.

They move through the next days with a shared awareness that doesn't announce itself. It hums beneath conversation, beneath routine, beneath the careful choices they keep making not to push, not to pull. Each decision feels provisional now, even the small ones.

Sera notices it when she reaches for a mug in the cabinet and pauses—Do I put it back where I always did? When she folds laundry and hesitates before tucking Beckett's shirt into the drawer she's been using, unsure if it's an assumption she's earned. When she drafts an email to Charleston and doesn't send it, then doesn't delete it either.

Everything feels like it's being held in a bracket.

Beckett feels it too. She sees it in the way he asks questions now—gentle, specific, carefully bounded. When are you meeting with the lawyer? instead of How long are you staying? Do you want to come out on the water tomorrow? instead of What are you doing next week?

He doesn't plan far ahead.

Neither does she.

They live inside the near future—the next meal, the next tide, the next errand into the village. It's a narrowing that feels both safe and brittle, like glass warmed just enough to bend but not enough to reshape.

At night, Sera lies awake listening to the sound of the island breathing—water shifting, insects starting and stopping, the house making its familiar complaints. She counts things she won't need to count later: how many times Beckett's truck passes the window before he parks, how long it takes the porch light to cool after it clicks off, the exact rhythm of his footsteps as he moves through rooms she's known her whole life.

She doesn't tell herself she's running out of time.

She tells herself she's being attentive.

But the difference grows thinner each night.

One afternoon, she watches Beckett loading gear into his truck, movements efficient, unhurried. He pauses once, hand resting on the tailgate, and looks toward the sound—not searching, just looking, the way someone does when they're imprinting a view they might not see the same way again.

The moment passes.

He climbs into the cab and drives off.

Sera stands in the yard long after the sound of the engine fades, the heat pressing down, the cicadas loud enough to feel intrusive. She thinks about how absence doesn't always arrive as departure. Sometimes it announces itself in advance, subtle and polite, asking only whether you're paying attention.

Later, at dinner, they talk about nothing that matters and everything that does. A neighbor's dock repair. The way the shrimp boats have been coming in earlier this season. A story from Beckett's childhood she's heard before but listens to differently now, aware of how stories change when you know they're finite.

She interrupts him once—not because she needs clarification, but because she doesn't want the moment to pass unmarked.

"What?" he asks, smiling.

"Nothing," she says. "I just—keep going."

He does.

But the interruption lingers between them, a small admission: I'm trying to hold this longer.

After dinner, they wash dishes together, not touching, not avoiding. Their reflections overlap faintly in the darkened window, two figures layered without fully merging. Sera watches the water run over Beckett's hands, the way it always does, and thinks about how time feels different when you're no longer assuming there's plenty of it.

She realizes then that this—this carefulness, this gentleness—isn't sustainable indefinitely.

Not because it's wrong.

Because it's temporary by design.

They both know it.

It's there in the way Beckett hesitates before making plans past the weekend. In the way Sera stops herself from buying groceries she won't use quickly. In the way they hold each other's gaze just a second too long, as if testing how much memory can be stored in a look.

The island reinforces it, quietly. The tides shifting earlier. The days shortening almost imperceptibly. The heat breaking just enough to signal that summer is moving toward something else.

Sera walks the shoreline alone one morning and notices how the waterline has changed again, how the sand bears fewer footprints than the day before. She understands then that erosion doesn't announce itself with collapse. It happens grain by grain, unnoticed until the edge is suddenly closer than expected.

When she returns to the house, Beckett is sitting on the steps, tying his boots. He looks up at her with that same steady presence, unchanged and yet entirely altered by what they both know.

"You okay?" he asks.

"Yes," she says. And it's true. "Are you?"

He nods. "Yeah."

Neither of them says what's thinning.

They don't need to.

The knowledge sits between them now—not as pressure, not yet—but as gravity.

And gravity, Sera knows, always gets its way.

He says it when the light is almost gone.

Not at sunset—that would feel too arranged—but in the thin blue after, when the beach has emptied and the island seems to draw itself inward. They're back at the house, shoes kicked off by the door, sand tracked halfway down the hall. The windows are open, letting in the sound of the marsh settling for the night.

Sera is rinsing her hands at the sink when she feels him behind her.

Not close.

Present.

"Can we talk for a minute?" he asks.

The phrasing is careful. Neutral. The kind of tone that doesn't brace for impact but doesn't soften either.

She turns off the faucet and nods. "Yeah."

They don't sit right away. That matters. Beckett stays standing, one hand resting lightly on the back of a chair, the other loose at his side. He's not blocking anything. Not pacing. Just anchored enough to speak without flinching.

"I've been thinking about what you said on the beach," he begins.

She waits.

"I don't want to rush you," he continues. "And I don't want to corner you into a decision that doesn't feel like yours."

Her chest tightens—not with fear, but recognition. He's naming the ground they've been standing on without pretending it's level.

"But," he adds quietly, "I can't keep living in the pause."

The word lands cleanly. Pause. Not limbo. Not waiting. Something temporary by definition.

She studies his face—the steadiness in it, the restraint. He isn't angry. He isn't wounded. He's resolved in a way that feels earned.

"I need you to hear this," he says, meeting her eyes. "Because if I don't say it now, I'll start resenting the quiet. And that's not fair to either of us."

She nods slowly. Her hands rest on the edge of the counter, fingers curled slightly, grounding herself.

"I'm not asking you to choose me," he says. "Or the island. Or anything permanent."

The care in the distinction almost breaks her.

"What I am asking," he continues, "is not to be something you fit around a decision you're not ready to make."

She inhales sharply. "I'm not trying to—"

"I know," he says gently, cutting her off without dismissing her. "I believe that. This isn't about intent."

He shifts his weight, the chair creaking softly beneath his hand. The sound feels too loud in the quiet kitchen.

"This place," he says, gesturing vaguely toward the window, the marsh beyond, "teaches you how to wait. I'm good at it. I've done it before."

Her pulse stutters.

"But waiting works only if there's movement underneath it," he goes on. "If it's headed somewhere."

She swallows. "And if it's not?"

"Then it becomes a way of disappearing slowly," he says. Not accusing. Naming.

The truth of it settles heavily between them.

She thinks of the days thinning. The careful restraint. The kiss held like glass. The way everything has begun to feel provisional, even kindness.

"I don't want to disappear," she says quietly.

"I know," he replies. "I just need to know that I'm not standing still while you figure out whether you're leaving."

Silence stretches.

Not empty.

Full.

Sera realizes then that this is Beckett at his most vulnerable—not pleading, not demanding, but refusing to bargain against himself. He's drawing a line not to control her, but to remain intact.

"What does that mean?" she asks.

He considers her for a moment, choosing precision over comfort.

"It means I won't keep acting like this is enough if it stops being honest," he says. "I won't punish you. I won't pull away to make a point. But I also won't keep building something that might be dismantled without a word."

Her throat tightens. "I wouldn't do that."

"I know you wouldn't mean to," he says. "That's the problem."

She closes her eyes briefly, absorbing the weight of it. When she opens them, she steps closer—not to touch, just to be nearer.

"So what happens now?" she asks.

He meets her gaze steadily. "Now we keep talking. Or we stop pretending this in-between can hold us."

The clarity of it feels like standing at low tide again, everything exposed, no water left to soften the edges.

Sera nods, slow and deliberate. "Temporary," she says, testing the word aloud.

Beckett's jaw tightens—not in anger, but resolve. "Temporary stopped working for me."

The sentence doesn't echo. It doesn't need to.

It settles.

Sera feels it land not as an ultimatum, but as a truth she can no longer skirt around. Temporary has carried her before—out of the island, into safety, into distance she mistook for strength.

But here, now, with Beckett standing solid and unyielding in his quiet way, temporary feels smaller than it used to.

Insufficient.

She exhales, a long breath she's been holding since the letter arrived, since the days began thinning, since the kiss became memory instead of momentum.

"I hear you," she says.

He nods once. "That's all I needed."

They stand there, the house breathing around them, the island settling into night. Nothing has been decided.

But something has ended.

Temporary—whatever safety it once offered—has become unacceptable.

Chapter Eight

The Breaking Point

The realtor arrives on a Wednesday, which feels like its own kind of insult.

Not a dramatic day. Not a day marked by grief anniversaries or storms or the house doing something particularly loud in its age. Just a weekday with clean sunlight and the persistent, ordinary sound of cicadas.

Sera hears the car before she sees it—tires on shell gravel, a deliberate slow roll up the drive as if the driver is already judging the angle of the porch and the state of the siding. The engine idles too smoothly. Not island-worn. Not salt-rattled.

She looks out through the kitchen window and sees a white SUV with tinted windows, the kind that stays clean because it doesn't park under live oaks or near marinas.

Her stomach drops.

Her body reacts with the same immediate, traitorous readiness it did when the letter arrived: shoulders lifting, breath tightening, hands going cold. She wipes her palms against her shorts without realizing it, leaving faint damp streaks on the fabric.

Practicality tries to assert itself.

Maybe she has the wrong address.

But the woman steps out with a clipboard and a bright, contained smile that says she does not.

She's dressed in crisp linen, sandals with a little heel that won't survive sand, hair pulled back neatly as if humidity is something that happens to other people. She pauses at the end of the walkway and scans the property with a practiced, appraising sweep: the porch, the roofline, the line of dunes, the marsh beyond. Her gaze lands on the old boat cradle in the yard and stays there a beat too long, already translating history into numbers.

Sera's throat tightens.

The house is behind her—warm, creaking, familiar. The woman out there is a future she hasn't chosen yet, arriving anyway.

Sera steps onto the porch and lets the screen door slap shut harder than necessary.

"Hello!" the realtor calls, voice bright, pitched to be friendly without being intimate. "Seraphina Lockwood?"

Sera forces her face into something neutral. "Yes."

"I'm Maren Cho," the woman says, walking up with her hand extended. "We spoke briefly on the phone last week—about scheduling a preliminary valuation? I was in the area and thought I'd stop by. Just to take a look at the exterior, no intrusion. It's so rare to get waterfront like this."

Sera doesn't remember speaking to her. Not really. She remembers the lawyer mentioning "someone who can give an estimate," remembers nodding while her mind was elsewhere, the way grief makes you agree to things simply to move through them.

Panic rises anyway.

Because "valuation" is not neutral.

It is a measuring.

A translation of her father's life into comparable sales and market desirability. A price tag placed on memory.

"I didn't realize you were coming today," Sera says, voice controlled.

Maren's smile doesn't falter. "Oh—I'm sorry. I sent an email yesterday. Sometimes service out here..." She gestures vaguely, as if the island's refusal to cooperate is quaint.

Sera's jaw clenches. "Right."

The realtor's gaze drifts again—toward the marsh, the dock, the line of sea oats. Sera can almost see the numbers flickering behind her eyes.

"You're going to have a lot of interest," Maren says. "Especially given recent demand. People want authenticity. Coastal character."

Coastal character.

Sera tastes the phrase like something metallic. The house isn't character. It's her father's hands. Her childhood. The place where her mother's absence first became a permanent weather system.

"Is Beckett here?" the realtor asks, flipping a page on her clipboard. "I was told there's a local contractor familiar with the property. It helps to have someone who knows the bones."

The question lands like a strike.

Beckett.

As if he's a utility. A credential. A local reference to make the sale smoother.

Sera's pulse hammers.

"He's working," she says, sharper than she intended.

Maren nods, undeterred. "No problem. I can walk the perimeter. Just take a few notes. I won't be in your way."

She starts down the steps before Sera can answer, already moving as if permission is implied. Sera follows, the heat thick on her skin, the world suddenly too bright.

They walk along the side of the house. Maren points out the roofline, the decking, the dune stabilization. She speaks in quick, confident phrases that reduce everything to condition and potential. Sera answers with minimal words, her mind splitting in two—one half hearing, one half flinching.

When Maren bends to inspect a foundation vent, Sera catches sight of Beckett's truck pulling up at the end of the drive.

Relief hits first—automatic.

Then dread.

Beckett gets out slowly. He takes in the scene in one glance: the white SUV, the clipboard, Sera's rigid posture. His expression doesn't change dramatically, but she sees the shift in his shoulders, the way his jaw tightens as if he's biting down on something.

He doesn't come closer.

That's what breaks her.

He pauses near the truck, as if choosing distance on purpose. His gaze meets hers once, steady and unreadable.

Maren straightens and turns with a bright smile that has no business being here. "Beckett Crowe? So nice to finally meet you. I've heard you're the one to call for—"

Beckett doesn't take her hand when she extends it. Not rudely. Just... not.

He nods once, curt. "Ma'am."

Maren laughs lightly, trying to smooth the moment. "I'm just doing a preliminary valuation. The property is gorgeous. I can already tell—"

Beckett's gaze moves past her, to the house. To the dock. To the sand-tracked steps. His voice is calm when he speaks, which makes it worse.

"You didn't tell me," he says to Sera.

The statement isn't accusation. It's fact.

Sera's mouth opens, closes. "I didn't—" She swallows. "I didn't schedule this. She just showed up."

Maren's smile falters slightly, sensing she's walked into something personal. "I can come back," she offers quickly. "Another time—"

"No," Beckett says, still calm. "Do what you came to do."

Sera flinches at the flatness of it.

Maren nods too many times, suddenly eager to retreat. "Of course. I'll... finish up and email you my notes." She gathers herself and moves toward her SUV with brisk, professional haste.

Sera watches her go, chest tight, the yard suddenly too quiet.

When the car finally pulls away, leaving only shell gravel settling back into place, Beckett is still by his truck.

Not coming closer.

Not closing the distance.

His restraint feels like a door closing softly.

Sera takes a step toward him. "Beckett—"

He lifts a hand slightly. Not to stop her, exactly. To ask for a beat. Space.

"Why is she here?" he asks, voice even.

Sera's panic flares again, but practicality tries to rescue her. "It's just an estimate," she says. "For the estate. I have to—there are legal things. Paperwork. I'm not selling tomorrow."

He nods once. "I know."

And yet.

His eyes don't soften.

"What I don't know," he says, "is why it feels like everything keeps moving toward leaving, even when you say you haven't decided."

The words land in her ribs.

"I'm trying to handle what needs handling," she says, voice tightening. "This house—my dad—none of that stops because I'm confused."

"I'm not asking you to stop," he replies. "I'm asking you to see what it looks like from where I'm standing."

Sera's hands curl into fists at her sides. She forces them open.

He takes a breath. His gaze drifts toward the sound, toward the marsh that has witnessed every coming and going on this island.

"Do you know what it felt like," he says quietly, "to watch a stranger walk around this place like it's a product?"

Sera swallows hard. "I didn't want her here."

"But she was," he says. Still calm. Still measured. "And that's the thing. Wanting and choosing aren't the same."

Her chest aches, sharp. "Beckett, I'm here."

"For now," he says.

The phrase isn't cruel. It's accurate.

Sera feels something in her crack—not shatter. Crack. A fissure opening under the weight of being seen too clearly.

"I'm not trying to leave you," she whispers.

He looks at her then, really looks. The steadiness in his eyes makes her throat burn.

"I'm not saying you're trying," he says. "I'm saying love without commitment feels like leaving anyway."

The sentence is quiet.

It ruptures something all the same.

Beckett's hand grips the edge of his truck bed for a moment—knuckles whitening—then releases.

"I can't do this part," he says. "The part where I start getting erased in advance."

Sera steps closer instinctively. "You're not—"

He shakes his head once. Not angry. Final.

"I'm going to the marina," he says. "I need space."

The words are plain, but the meaning is brutal: he's stepping away to stay whole.

He climbs into his truck. The engine turns over. He backs out slowly, gravel crunching under tires, the sound too loud in the sudden quiet.

Sera stands in the yard as the truck disappears down the road, the heat pressing in, the house looming behind her like a witness.

The sky remains clear.

No storm to match the rupture.

Just the steady, relentless sound of the island—water moving, wind shifting, time continuing.

The marina smells like diesel and salt and sun-warmed rope.

It's a smell Sera has known her whole life, one that used to mean afternoons spent waiting on the dock with her feet dangling above green water, counting pelicans and pretending she wasn't watching for a particular boat. Today it feels sharper.

More exposed. Like standing under bright lights with nowhere to look but straight ahead.

She finds Beckett at the far end of the docks, where the slips open toward the sound and the water runs darker and deeper. His boat is tied up alongside, rocking gently against the pilings, lines creaking with the tide. He's standing on the dock, back to her, hands busy with a knot he doesn't actually need to redo.

The decision to come here wasn't planned.

It arrived the way most of her hardest choices do—not as resolve, but as discomfort she couldn't sit with any longer. The space he took earlier didn't feel like abandonment. It felt like an invitation she hadn't answered yet.

She walks slowly, the boards warm beneath her sandals, every step loud in the open air. Gulls argue overhead. Somewhere nearby, an engine coughs and then catches. Life continuing, indifferent.

Beckett doesn't turn when she stops a few feet behind him.

She knows he's aware of her anyway. He always is.

"I didn't mean for today to happen like that," she says.

The words come out steadier than she feels.

He finishes the knot before answering. Tests it with a tug. Only then does he turn to face her.

"I know," he says.

Not forgiveness.

Not absolution.

Understanding.

It almost hurts more.

She gestures vaguely back toward the village, the house, the driveway where the white SUV idled. "I wasn't ready. I still don't know what I'm doing."

"I know that too," he says.

The water laps softly against the dock, the sound rhythmic and patient. Beckett rests one hand on a piling, grounding himself. He doesn't step closer. He doesn't step back.

They stand in the open like this, nothing between them but weather and truth.

"What I didn't expect," she says carefully, "was how fast it would feel like I was already leaving."

Beckett's jaw tightens, just slightly. He looks out over the sound, eyes narrowed against the glare. "That's because leaving doesn't start when you pack a bag."

The words land clean and precise.

She swallows. "I'm not trying to erase you."

"I know," he repeats. Then, after a beat, "But intention doesn't change impact."

The phrase settles heavily between them.

Sera steps closer, the edge of the dock creaking under her weight. "This place—this house—it's tied up in so much. My dad. My mom. Everything I never finished dealing with."

He nods once. "I get that."

"And you're tied up in it too," she adds, quieter now. "Whether that's fair or not."

He looks at her then, really looks. The steadiness in his gaze makes her chest ache.

"That's the part I need to be honest about," he says. "I can hold a lot. I can wait through storms, through seasons. But I can't be something you carry while you decide whether you're staying."

Her breath catches. "I'm not asking you to be."

"Maybe not out loud," he says gently. "But that's what it feels like."

The dock shifts slightly as a boat passes, wake rippling outward. Sera steadies herself instinctively, fingers curling around the rough wood of a piling. The texture bites into her skin, grounding her.

"I'm scared," she admits suddenly.

The word slips free before she can temper it.

Beckett's expression changes—not softening exactly, but sharpening into focus. "Of what?"

She laughs once, brittle. "Of choosing wrong. Of staying and resenting it. Of leaving and realizing too late what I lost."

He considers her for a long moment. The marina hums around them—voices, engines, water moving through space.

"You know what scares me?" he asks quietly.

She shakes her head.

"That I become a place you pass through," he says. "Not even intentionally. Just because I was here when you needed shelter."

The honesty of it hits her low and hard.

"That's not what you are to me," she says.

"I believe you," he replies. "But belief doesn't erase pattern."

The words sting because they're earned.

She takes another step closer. This time, he doesn't stop her. The space between them closes until she can feel the heat of him, the familiar steadiness that has always made the world feel more navigable.

"I don't want to lose you," she says.

He exhales slowly, a sound that holds years of restraint. "I don't want to lose myself waiting."

The wind shifts off the water, carrying the smell of salt deeper into the marina. Flags snap softly on their lines. Somewhere, a bell clangs once and then settles.

They stand there, close now but not touching, the dock holding them both as if it understands the weight of what's happening.

"I'm not ready to promise anything," she says, voice tight.

"I know," he says.

"But I'm not ready to say goodbye either."

He meets her gaze, something like sadness flickering there—not defeat, not anger. Recognition.

"Then this is where we pause," he says. "Not because we don't care. Because we do."

The word pause feels different here than it did before. Heavier. More defined.

She nods, throat burning. "I don't want this to be the end."

"It's not," he says. "But it can't keep being halfway."

She understands then that this confrontation isn't about the house or the realtor or even the island.

It's about visibility.

About whether love that refuses commitment is still love—or simply a quieter form of leaving.

The dock creaks beneath them as another boat rocks past, water slapping wood. Beckett steps back, just one pace, reclaiming the space he needs to remain whole.

"I need to step away from this," he says. "Not because I don't want you. Because I do."

The distinction matters.

She watches him untie the last line, movements efficient, practiced. He isn't running. He isn't shutting her out.

He's choosing himself.

And as she stands there on the dock, the sound opening wide in front of her, Sera realizes that the rupture has arrived—not as explosion, but as clarity.

The relationship hasn't been destroyed.

But it has been broken open, and there's no way to pretend otherwise now.

The weather doesn't rise to meet the moment.

That, more than anything, makes it unbearable.

The sky remains an unbroken blue, bleached slightly by afternoon heat. The sound is calm, almost polite—water lapping against hulls, halyards ticking softly against aluminum masts, a gull's cry drifting lazily overhead. No storm gathers. No wind kicks up to dramatize the rupture.

The island does not perform grief on her behalf.

Sera stands on the dock long after Beckett's boat has cleared the marina, the wake flattening into nothing as if it never existed. The absence he leaves behind is not loud. It doesn't echo.

It settles.

She becomes acutely aware of the space her body occupies now—how much air surrounds her, how far the end of the dock feels from the beginning. The boards beneath her feet are warm and steady, unchanged by what has just happened. That steadiness feels almost cruel.

She listens.

A distant engine hums. Someone laughs farther down the marina. A cooler lid slams shut. Life continues in recognizable rhythms, each sound reinforcing the same truth: the world has not paused for her fracture.

She walks slowly toward the end of the dock, each step measured, the creak of wood registering like a metronome. The sound follows her, marking movement without urgency. She stops where the dock meets open water and grips the railing, knuckles whitening briefly before she forces herself to loosen them.

The water is darker here, deeper, less reflective. It moves steadily, small ripples catching light and then losing it. The sound is constant and indifferent, the way it has always been.

This is what separation looks like without spectacle.

She thinks of storms—the way they announce themselves on Hatteras, the way the air thickens and birds vanish and the horizon darkens like a held breath. She's always known how to read those signs. Known when to prepare, when to retreat, when to wait it out.

This offers no such guidance.

There is no warning system for the quiet ending of something unfinished.

She presses her forehead briefly against the cool metal railing, closing her eyes. The heat presses in from all sides, unrelieved. Sweat beads at the base of her neck. She lets it happen, refuses the impulse to wipe it away.

Discomfort, she reminds herself. Stay with it.

The sounds around her sharpen. The rhythmic slap of water against pilings. The faint whistle of wind through rigging. Somewhere, a radio plays low and tinny, the melody indistinct but persistent.

She realizes then that Beckett's departure didn't rupture the day.

It redefined it.

Before, time had felt thin but continuous—stretchable, malleable. Now it feels segmented. There is before the marina and after the marina. The difference is subtle but absolute.

She turns back toward shore.

The walk feels longer this time. The dock hasn't changed length, but her awareness has shifted. Each step away from the water feels like an acknowledgment of distance, a confirmation that space—once claimed—does not simply collapse again.

At the parking lot, the heat rises off the asphalt in visible waves. She squints against the glare, suddenly aware of how exposed she feels in daylight. No shadows deep enough to hide in. No dusk to soften edges.

Her car sits where she left it, dusted lightly with sand. The ordinariness of it feels wrong. She opens the door, sits for a moment without starting the engine, hands resting uselessly in her lap.

She listens again.

The marina fades behind her as she pulls onto the road, replaced by the steady hum of tires on pavement. Windows down, salt air rushes in, warm and relentless. The marsh slips past in shades of green and gold, the grasses bending slightly, obedient to a breeze too light to matter.

The island looks the same.

That's the hardest part.

The house comes into view slowly, rising out of familiar landscape like it always has. The porch. The steps. The yard where her father once worked, where Beckett stood earlier and chose space instead of closeness.

She parks and sits again, longer this time.

The screen door creaks when she pushes it open. The sound lands in the quiet house like an accusation, though she knows it isn't one. The interior smells faintly of wood and old salt and coffee grounds. Nothing has been disturbed.

She moves through rooms carefully, as if something fragile has been laid across every surface.

In the bedroom, the bed is made—too neatly. Beckett's pillow remains where it always was, indentation smoothed but not erased. The sight of it hits her low in the chest.

Physical separation, she realizes, isn't only about distance.

It's about objects that haven't caught up yet.

She steps back onto the porch as evening begins to lean toward late afternoon. The light shifts almost imperceptibly, warming, flattening. A breeze finally picks up—not enough to cool her, just enough to move the wind chimes her father hung years ago.

They sound once.

Then again.

The notes are uneven, familiar. They don't align into melody. They never have.

She sits on the top step, elbows on her knees, watching the marsh as it darkens slightly, the water threading through it with quiet persistence. The tide continues its cycle, unconcerned with human timing.

This, too, is a mirror.

Things don't end all at once.

They change state.

Sera understands now that what has broken between her and Beckett isn't affection or history or even possibility. Those remain, stubborn and intact.

What has broken is the illusion that they could keep standing in the same place indefinitely without consequence.

Erasure isn't dramatic. It doesn't announce itself. It happens quietly, in the negative space where intention and impact fail to meet. It happens when you keep someone close enough to feel real, but never close enough to be chosen.

She has spent years believing abandonment defined her—the sharpness of being left without explanation. A mother who disappeared so completely that memory felt unreliable. A father who stayed but retreated inward.

What she hasn't wanted to examine is what it feels like to be the one who leaves without meaning to.

She has mistaken ambiguity for gentleness.

She has mistaken restraint for safety.

And she has mistaken her own fear of being left for proof that she is incapable of leaving others behind.

The truth sits heavy and unavoidable: loving someone without choosing them isn't neutrality.

It's erosion.

The separation is real. It has shape. It has weight.

But it is not annihilation.

The island holds its breath around her, not in warning, not in comfort—just in witness.

The relationship is broken.

Not destroyed.

And standing there in the steady, unremarkable weather, Sera knows with a clarity that aches but does not collapse her: broken things can still be mended.

They just cannot be returned to what they were before.

Sera must now choose.

Chapter Nine

What the Island Asks

She leaves the house before the day fully decides what it is.

Not at dawn—that would feel like ceremony—but in the early hour when the light is still thin and the air carries the cool trace of night. The porch boards are damp under her bare feet. Somewhere in the marsh, a heron lifts with a slow, irritated flap, as if disturbed by her movement.

Sera doesn't bring anything with her. No phone. No water bottle. No keys beyond what she needs to lock the door behind her.

She tells herself it's because she'll only be gone a little while.

The truth is simpler: she doesn't want distraction. She doesn't want a tether back to the kind of thinking that loops in circles. She wants the island to speak without interruption.

The road is quiet as she walks the short distance toward the beach access, sand already creeping across the asphalt in thin drifts. The sea oats along the dune line move with a soft, constant rustle. Even in still air, they sound like they're whispering to each other.

Her body remembers this walk.

Not the exact steps, but the feeling of it—the slight incline as the path climbs, the way the dunes hide the ocean until the last moment, forcing you to earn the view. She climbs without hurrying, palms brushing the wooden railing where it's been smoothed by years of hands.

At the crest, the Atlantic opens in front of her.

Not dramatic. Not violent. Just present.

The water rolls in steady lines, gray-blue under the morning sky, the surface textured by wind she can't quite feel yet but can see in the way the waves feather at their edges. The horizon looks close and unreachable at the same time, a clean line that doesn't bend for anyone.

She steps onto the beach.

The sand here is cool, packed firm by the outgoing tide. Each footprint holds its shape for a moment before the next breath of wind softens it. The air smells sharp—salt and wet sand and the faint metallic tang that always clings to the edge of the ocean. It fills her lungs in a way that feels like it's clearing something out.

She starts walking south, toward the long, familiar curve of Hatteras shoreline. Toward where the dunes rise and fall like shoulders. Toward the places that used to feel like home and now feel like questions.

The beach is almost empty.

A fisherman stands far down near the waterline, casting into the surf with patient, repetitive motion. Two pelicans skim low over the waves, wings barely moving, their shadows sliding across the water. Closer to her, ghost crab holes pock the sand near the dune edge, tiny and precise. A few shells lie scattered in the wrack line—bits of whelk and coquina, a sand dollar cracked cleanly in half.

She finds herself cataloging the details the way she always does when she's trying not to think.

But the island doesn't let her stay in the shallow part of herself for long.

The dunes pull her attention. The sea oats. The way the sand has shifted since she last walked here, reshaping familiar contours. A section of dune face looks freshly cut, the slope sharper than she remembers, as if the last storm took a bite and left the wound exposed.

She climbs a little higher along the edge where the sand is softer, her calves tightening with the effort. The wind is stronger up here. It threads through her hair, lifts it off her neck, cools the places that still feel too warm inside her.

From the dune line, she can see more.

The sweep of beach, the scattered houses set back behind sea grass, the thin thread of road. The sound on the other side of the island isn't visible from here, but she can feel it anyway—water on both sides, the narrowness of land holding its shape between forces that never stop pressing.

This is what she came back to.

A place that is never settled.

A place that survives by yielding.

She walks along the ridge for a while, letting the dune crest guide her. Sea oats brush her thighs, soft but insistent. Their seed heads nod in the wind, tiny weights at the end of slender stems, bending without breaking.

Her thoughts, uninvited, drift toward Beckett.

The way his voice sounded when he said he needed to step away. The steadiness. The refusal to turn the moment into spectacle. The space he left behind, clean and defined, like a boundary drawn with a ruler.

She feels it in her body now—an absence that has weight.

Not loneliness.

A missing pressure. A missing warmth at her back. A missing presence that used to make the world feel steadier just by standing near her.

She stops without meaning to, one hand lifting to her chest as if she can physically locate what's been removed.

The ocean keeps rolling in.

The gulls keep calling.

The fisherman keeps casting.

The island does not shift to accommodate her grief.

It witnesses.

It's always done that—held her in full view without offering comfort beyond what is real: wind, water, sand, the slow truth of time.

Sera sits on the slope of a dune, sand sliding under her as she settles. She draws her knees up, wraps her arms around them, and watches the tide line.

It's going out right now. Pulling back. Revealing darker sand beneath, leaving behind glistening strips of wet shore. The sea gives and takes in quiet increments, never asking permission, never explaining itself.

She watches a wave break and recede, foam thinning into lace, and something in her chest loosens—not relief, not resolution, just a small widening.

If she stays here long enough, she thinks, the tide will turn.

It always turns.

She doesn't know what she'll do with that yet.

But she knows—sitting alone on a dune on Hatteras Island, wind in her hair, salt on her lips—that the island will remain what it is.

And so will she.

For now, she simply stays where she is, letting the morning hold her in plain sight, letting the shoreline keep moving while something quieter inside her begins to take shape.

She doesn't remember the exact moment her mother left.

That's the first truth that surfaces as she sits there on the dune, sand pressing into the backs of her thighs, the ocean breathing in front of her like it always has. There is no single image she can point to and say this was it. No slammed door. No shouted goodbye. No cinematic fracture.

Her mother's leaving was quieter than that.

It arrived the way absence often does on the island—gradually, and then all at once.

Sera remembers the before with sharp clarity. Her mother's bare feet on the porch boards in the early morning, the way she tied her hair up with whatever was closest—rubber band, strip of cloth, nothing at all. The sound of her humming while she rinsed sand out of their swimsuits at the outdoor spigot. The way she stood at the water's edge, arms crossed loosely, watching the tide as if it might answer her back.

She remembers thinking her mother belonged to the island in a way other people didn't.

Not rooted, exactly.

Attuned.

Her mother moved like someone always listening for something just out of reach. A shift in wind. A change in weather. A call only she could hear.

The leaving didn't come with warning, but in hindsight, the signs were everywhere.

Longer walks alone along the sound side. Silence where conversation used to live. The way her mother's gaze lingered on the horizon, not longing, not quite sadness—more like evaluation. As if she were measuring a distance she intended to cross.

Sera remembers one afternoon in particular.

She would have been eleven, maybe twelve. Old enough to notice patterns, too young to understand them. The heat had been thick, the kind that pressed sweat into the small of her back even in the shade. Her father was in the shed, working on a hull, the steady rhythm of hammer on wood echoing across the yard.

Her mother sat at the kitchen table, hands folded, staring at nothing.

Sera had asked if she was okay.

Her mother smiled—soft, distracted—and said, Of course.

That smile comes back to her now with unsettling clarity.

Not reassurance.

Permission.

The day her mother left, Sera remembers the house being unnaturally quiet. No radio playing. No hum of conversation from room to room. The air felt paused, like the moment before a storm when the birds disappear and even the cicadas fall silent.

Her mother wasn't there.

Her father stood at the counter, one hand braced against the edge, the other holding a note so thin it looked like it might dissolve if he breathed on it too hard. He didn't read it aloud. He didn't need to.

Sera knew.

Not the reasons. Not the details.

Just the fact of it.

Her mother had gone.

What she remembers most vividly isn't the panic she expected to feel, but the way her body went still. As if some instinct had told her movement would make the loss more real. She remembers standing in the doorway, watching her father's shoulders slump just slightly, and thinking—This is what staying costs.

They never talked about it much after that.

Her father didn't curse her mother's name. He didn't romanticize her departure either. He simply continued on, day after day, working, fixing, existing in the shape she left behind. He stayed in the house. He stayed on the island. He stayed with Sera.

Staying, she learned, could be an act of endurance rather than choice.

And leaving, she learned, could look like self-preservation even when it fractured everything in its path.

Sera turns her face into the wind now, eyes closing briefly as it pushes hair across her cheek. The memory sits heavier than she expected—not sharp, but layered. Complicated. Alive.

She understands her mother better now than she ever did then.

The island doesn't let you disappear quietly. It presses in. It asks things of you. It demands attention, presence, resilience. Some people rise to that.

Others feel themselves thinning.

Her mother didn't leave because she didn't love them.

She left because loving them here felt like a kind of erasure.

That realization settles into Sera's chest with a dull ache.

Because she recognizes it.

The pattern isn't just inherited.

It's rehearsed.

She has told herself her whole adult life that leaving is a way to survive. That distance equals clarity. That departure is neutral, not violent. That people will understand.

And they do.

Until they don't.

Until staying behind becomes its own kind of wound.

The ocean shifts in front of her, a wave breaking harder than the ones before it, white water rushing farther up the sand before retreating again. She tracks its movement automatically, breath syncing without conscious effort.

Her mother left without explanation.

Her father stayed without complaint.

Sera has spent years trying to live somewhere in between.

But sitting here now, with the island steady and unyielding around her, she understands something she didn't before:

Avoidance isn't neutrality.

It is a decision.

One that echoes.

She opens her eyes and watches the water pull back, leaving the sand darker and smooth where it passed. The tide continues its work, indifferent to memory, to inheritance, to intention.

The island remembers anyway.

And for the first time, Sera lets herself remember too—not to justify leaving, not to condemn staying, but to see the shape of the choice she's been circling all along.

Her father's staying was never dramatic.

That's what distinguishes it most sharply in her memory—not as an act of bravery or sacrifice, but as something quieter and more relentless. He did not announce it. He did not defend it. He simply remained, day after day, as if absence were a condition that could be absorbed by routine.

After her mother left, the house did not change its rhythms right away.

The coffee still brewed at the same hour. The radio still played low in the mornings, tuned to the same local station that faded in and out depending on the weather. Her father still rose before the sun, pulled on his work boots, and crossed the yard toward the shed with the same measured pace.

Staying, Sera learned, could look indistinguishable from habit.

At first, she thought he stayed because he didn't know how to leave. That the island had closed around him, made the idea of anywhere else feel impossible. She told herself this because it made his grief easier to understand. Easier to forgive.

But as the years passed, she began to see the choice underneath.

Her father knew exactly what leaving looked like.

He had watched it happen.

He had read the note in his hand and felt the air collapse around him. He had stood in the same kitchen she stands in now and understood that staying would not undo what had been taken.

And still, he stayed.

Sera remembers afternoons in the boat shed after her mother was gone. The air thick with sawdust and heat, the smell of resin sharp enough to sting her eyes. Her father worked methodically, planing wood smooth, checking measurements twice, correcting small imperfections no one else would notice.

She would sit on an overturned bucket nearby, swinging her legs, watching the slow precision of his hands.

Once, she asked him why he didn't sell the house.

The question came out smaller than she intended. Casual, even. As if she were asking about paint color or weather.

He paused, the plane still in his hands, fingers curled around the worn handle. He didn't look at her right away.

"This place still works," he said finally.

She waited, sensing there was more.

"For me," he added.

That answer frustrated her then. It felt incomplete. Evasive.

Now, it feels devastatingly honest.

The island worked for him—not because it healed him, but because it gave his grief somewhere to exist without explanation. The work of tides. The slow repair of broken things. The understanding that not everything lost could be replaced, but some things could still be made sound again.

Her father did not stay because he believed her mother would return.

He stayed because leaving would have meant abandoning the life he chose after she was gone.

That distinction matters.

Sera shifts her weight on the dune, sand sliding beneath her, and lets the thought settle. The ocean continues its steady motion below, waves stacking and releasing with patient inevitability.

Her father stayed and raised her alone.

Not heroically. Not bitterly.

Just thoroughly.

He packed her lunches. He learned how to braid her hair badly enough that she eventually took over. He attended school meetings smelling faintly of varnish and salt. He listened more than he spoke. He let her ask questions he couldn't answer without flinching.

He never spoke poorly of her mother.

But he never pretended her leaving was painless either.

There were nights she heard him moving through the house long after she'd gone to bed, footsteps measured, the screen door opening and closing as he stepped out onto the porch to sit with his thoughts. There were mornings when his eyes looked older than the rest of him, as if sleep had not been kind.

Staying took something from him.

And he accepted that cost.

Sera realizes now that this was the lesson he never articulated but lived every day: that love does not disappear simply because someone leaves, and that staying does not guarantee safety or ease.

It guarantees responsibility.

Her chest tightens at the thought.

Because she has always believed responsibility was the thing that would undo her.

She told herself she left places before they could trap her. That movement was freedom. That staying too long was how you vanished.

But watching her father all those years, she missed the other truth:

Staying is not the opposite of leaving.

It is a separate act entirely.

One that requires endurance, yes—but also presence. Attention. A willingness to remain visible even when it would be easier to fade out of your own life.

Her father stayed on Hatteras Island knowing exactly what it would cost him.

He stayed anyway.

Sera looks back toward the dunes, toward the narrow strip of land that holds a house full of echoes and a man who just stepped away because he refused to become another silent endurance.

She understands now that Beckett's boundary is not a rejection of love.

It is a refusal to repeat her father's quiet erasure.

The realization doesn't bring comfort.

But it brings clarity.

Her father chose staying as an act of commitment—to place, to work, to her.

Her mother chose leaving as an act of survival.

And Sera has spent years believing she could avoid choosing at all.

The tide shifts below her, subtle but unmistakable, the water beginning its slow return toward shore. She watches the line advance, knowing it will reach the place she sits if she waits long enough.

For the first time, she does not move away.

She sits with the knowledge that staying and leaving are both costs, and that the real danger has always been pretending otherwise.

The island does not move closer to her.

That is the first thing she notices when she lifts her head from the tangle of memory and looks around again. The dunes remain where they are. The ocean keeps its distance. The sky does not soften or darken in response to her thinking. Nothing leans in to soothe her.

The island does not comfort.

It observes.

Wind threads steadily through the sea oats, bending them just enough to show their flexibility without breaking their spines. Sand skitters across the surface of the dune in thin, restless lines, rearranging itself grain by grain. The sound of the surf stays constant—neither louder nor quieter than before—each wave following the last with quiet discipline.

This place has never been sentimental.

Sera has always known that, even when she tried to pretend otherwise. As a child, she mistook familiarity for affection. She believed the island loved her because it held her, because it allowed her to run barefoot without consequence, because it shaped her days with such clarity.

Now she understands the difference.

The island does not love.

It endures.

She watches a piece of driftwood rock in the shallows, rolling slightly with each incoming wave before settling again. It has been smoothed by years of motion, edges rounded, surface bleached nearly white. Whatever sharpness it once had is gone—not erased, but transformed by repetition.

Witness, not intervention.

That is the island's role.

It watched her mother walk away without lifting a hand to stop her. It watched her father stay and shoulder the long work of aftermath. It watched Sera herself leave and return and leave again, never asking for explanation, never offering absolution.

The dunes bear the marks of past storms—cuts and collapses that haven't fully healed, layers of sand reformed but visibly altered. She traces one of those lines with her eyes now, the way the slope dips and then rises again, uneven but stable.

This is what survival looks like here.

Not restoration.

Adaptation.

The island has always made its terms clear. It does not promise safety. It does not guarantee permanence. Houses shift. Shorelines retreat. Roads flood and are rebuilt. What remains is not what was, but what managed to hold its shape long enough to matter.

Sera presses her palm into the sand beside her, feeling the grit work its way into her skin. The sensation is grounding in its honesty. Sand doesn't pretend to be anything else. It yields when pressure is applied. It leaves its mark in return.

She thinks of all the times she's come to this beach looking for reassurance. For permission. For some sign that she was doing the right thing by leaving, by staying away, by refusing to anchor herself too deeply to any one place or person.

The island never gave her that.

It gave her continuity instead.

A reminder that time moves whether you choose or not.

That erosion happens quietly.

That neglect and patience can look the same from a distance.

A gust of wind lifts, stronger now, snapping the sea oats and sending a shiver through her. She draws her arms tighter around herself, not cold exactly, but aware of exposure. The sun is higher, the light sharpening, stripping softness from the landscape.

This is daylight truth.

Nothing is obscured.

The fisherman down the beach has moved farther away, his figure reduced to silhouette against the water. The pelicans have disappeared. A lone sandpiper darts along the shore, quick and precise, chasing something too small for her to see.

Life continues in fragments.

The island bears witness to all of it without hierarchy.

It does not privilege love over loss, staying over leaving, intention over impact. It records everything in layers—sand over sand, water over water—without commentary.

Sera realizes this is why the island has always felt dangerous to her in ways she couldn't name.

It does not allow selective memory.

You cannot curate your history here. You cannot soften it with distance or reshape it with narrative. The island remembers storms long after the sky clears. It remembers foundations that shifted, even when the house above looks intact.

It remembers who stayed.

It remembers who left.

And it remembers who stood in between, hoping not to be seen choosing at all.

She exhales slowly, the breath catching just slightly at the end. Her body has begun to respond to the truth her mind has been circling for days now. A heaviness in her limbs. A settling behind her ribs.

The island does not absolve her.

But it does not condemn her either.

It offers something harder.

Clarity.

Sera sits with that, letting the wind move around her, letting the sound of the surf mark time without meaning. She understands now that the comfort she's been seeking here was never part of the bargain.

What the island offers is perspective.

A wide enough view to see patterns.

A long enough memory to expose them.

She closes her eyes briefly, not to escape, but to listen more closely—to the steady breath of the ocean, to the wind combing the dunes, to the quiet, relentless presence of a place that has never asked her to be anything but honest.

When she opens them again, the island is unchanged.

And neither, she knows, is she.

Not yet.

But the witness has been given.

She doesn't arrive at the truth all at once.

It comes in increments, the way the island itself reveals damage—not with collapse, but with exposure. A line of erosion made visible only when the tide pulls back far enough. A foundation sound until you notice the way the porch leans, just slightly, away from square.

Sera watches her own thoughts the way she's learned to watch weather.

She knows the familiar movements. The instinctive reach for distance when something begins to matter. The mental inventory of exits. The quiet relief that follows the decision to leave before leaving becomes necessary.

She has always called this prudence.

She has always believed it made her careful.

Sitting here now, with the island offering no distraction, she lets the word escape surface without pushing it away.

It doesn't feel dramatic when she names it.

It feels accurate.

She thinks of Charleston—the way she curated her life there with intention. The apartment with its clean lines and controlled light. The job that asked for precision but not presence. Relationships shaped around convenience and plausible deniability. She was admired for her composure, her independence, her ability to move on without fuss.

No one ever accused her of being unreliable.

They just stopped asking her to stay.

She realizes now how often she has mistaken departure for agency. How easily she framed leaving as a decision made for herself rather than a refusal to remain accountable to the discomfort of being known.

It wasn't that she didn't love.

It was that she left before love could demand something back.

The pattern becomes unmistakable once she allows herself to see it.

She leaves places right as they begin to ask for continuity. She leaves people when desire edges too close to vulnerability. She leaves conversations unfinished because finishing them would require clarity she's not ready to provide.

She leaves so she doesn't have to say no.

She leaves so she doesn't have to say yes either.

Sera presses her thumb into the pad of her forefinger, grounding herself in the small sting of pressure. The ocean rolls on, indifferent to her inventory. The wind lifts again, carrying sand that skims across the dune and taps against her bare ankle.

She remembers the ease with which she left Beckett years ago.

Not the pain—she remembers that too—but the justification. The narrative she constructed so quickly it felt like truth: I need to find myself. This place is too small. I'll come back when I'm ready.

Ready for what?

She never answered that.

She didn't need to. Leaving allowed her to postpone the question indefinitely.

The realization tightens her chest—not with guilt exactly, but with recognition. She has been rehearsing this pattern since childhood, refining it, making it socially acceptable. Her mother left because staying felt like erasure. Her father stayed because leaving would have erased something else.

Sera learned from both.

And from neither completely.

She has been leaving not to survive, but to avoid choosing what survival would require.

The island makes this impossible to ignore.

Because here, every path loops back on itself. Every road ends in water. You cannot move forward without eventually encountering the limits of land.

She laughs softly under her breath—not humor, but acknowledgment. The sound is swallowed by the wind.

She thinks of Beckett again, but this time without the ache she's been nursing. She thinks of him as a mirror rather than a wound. The way he offered closeness without demand. The way he stepped back not to punish her, but to preserve himself.

He named a boundary she has spent years skirting.

Temporary is not enough.

The words land differently now.

Not as pressure.

As diagnosis.

She understands that she has made a career out of temporary. Of provisional lives. Of arrangements that allow her to feel wanted without being required.

Naming the pattern doesn't break it.

But it gives it shape.

And shape is something she can no longer pretend not to see.

The tide has begun to turn.

She notices it not by looking at the water directly, but by the way the wet line creeps closer to her feet. The sand beneath her shifts slightly, becoming cooler, denser. The ocean does not rush back in. It advances patiently, almost politely.

The island does not force decisions.

It reveals consequences.

Sera draws a slow breath, then another, feeling the air fill her lungs more deeply than it has in days. She lets the recognition settle without rushing to resolve it.

She has always been good at departure.

What she has never practiced is staying long enough to be altered by the choice.

That knowledge does not instruct her yet.

It simply waits.

Clear, unavoidable, and no longer deniable.

The absence does not announce itself as loneliness.

It arrives as imbalance.

Sera notices it first in the way her body keeps orienting toward a presence that isn't there. The subtle turn of her shoulders as if making space for someone to stand beside her. The unconscious slowing of her pace, calibrated for a stride that used to match her own. Even the way her breath seems to pause at the top of an inhale, waiting for another rhythm to sync with.

Her body remembers before her mind does.

She shifts on the dune, sand whispering beneath her weight, and feels the place beside her where someone might sit. The absence has dimension. It takes up room. It presses lightly at her side, the way humidity does—unseen but undeniable.

She presses her palm to the sand again, then lifts it, brushing grains from her skin. The motion feels incomplete, like half a gesture abandoned mid-thought.

This is how she knows it's real.

Not because she misses him—missing would imply sentimentality she's not ready to claim—but because her body keeps accounting for him anyway.

She stands and resumes walking, letting the firm sand guide her closer to the waterline. The tide has turned enough now that the waves reach farther up the shore, darkening the sand with each slow advance. The water is cold where it touches her ankles, the shock sharp enough to draw her fully into the present.

She welcomes it.

The Atlantic has always been honest with her.

She walks until the water numbs her feet slightly, then stops, letting the waves circle her calves. The pull is gentle but insistent, a reminder that standing still requires effort. Balance is not passive.

She thinks of Beckett's hands.

Not the way they touched her, but the way they rested—open, patient, never demanding more than she offered. She remembers the steadiness of his presence at her back, the quiet heat that grounded her without asking her to lean.

She had thought she could take or leave that.

She understands now how wrong she was.

The absence sharpens her awareness of everything else. The way the wind pushes harder from the northeast, flattening the surface of the water. The grit of salt drying on her skin. The faint ache in her shoulders from holding herself upright without the subtle counterweight she didn't realize she'd been using.

Her chest tightens unexpectedly, not with pain exactly, but with recognition.

She has been living as if closeness were optional.

As if proximity were indulgence.

Her body tells a different story.

It has learned how to stand beside someone without surrender. It has learned how to rest against another presence without losing itself. And now, deprived of that calibration, it feels slightly off-kilter—like a boat freed from its mooring, drifting just enough to be noticeable.

She steps back out of the water and walks north again, shoes in hand, the wet sand squeaking faintly underfoot. The sound is oddly intimate, amplified by the quiet beach. Each step announces itself, unavoidable.

She wonders how many times Beckett has walked this same stretch alone.

The thought lands low in her chest.

She imagines him noticing the same details—the angle of the light, the way the dunes cast shallow shadows, the faint line of shells marking where the tide has been. She imagines his body adjusting to the space she left behind, his steps recalibrating the same way hers are now.

The symmetry unsettles her.

She realizes then that absence is not neutral.

It is felt differently depending on where you stand.

Her phone, forgotten in the house, does not vibrate with messages she pretends not to want. No one interrupts her thoughts. The silence is total enough to feel curated.

She resists the urge to break it.

Instead, she lets the absence continue its quiet work.

It settles in her shoulders, reminding her of the way she leaned against him without thinking. It tightens briefly at her throat when she remembers the sound of his voice close to her ear—low, steady, never raised. It lingers at her back, a ghost pressure where his hand once rested, not possessive, just present.

The realization is not that she needs him.

It's that she allowed herself to be with him.

And that allowance has altered her internal landscape.

The island bears witness without commentary.

A gull lands a short distance away, pecks at something in the sand, then lifts again. The fisherman she noticed earlier is gone now, leaving behind only faint footprints that the tide is already erasing.

Everything leaves traces.

Everything is erased.

Sera slows, then stops, standing alone at the edge of the water with the wind pulling at her hair. She closes her eyes, not to retreat, but to catalog the sensations—the pull of gravity, the press of air, the steady drum of her own heart.

She has spent years believing she could move through the world without leaving marks.

Without being marked in return.

The absence of Beckett disproves that.

It is not dramatic. It does not demand. It simply exists, shaping her awareness in ways she cannot ignore.

She opens her eyes and looks down the length of the beach again, the horizon stretching clean and uncompromising ahead of her.

The space beside her remains empty.

And for the first time, she does not rush to fill it—or to flee from it.

She stands there long enough to feel what that absence is asking of her.

Not action.

Recognition.

The clarity settles quietly, as steady and unavoidable as the tide at her feet.

The decision does not arrive as a sentence.

It doesn't say stay or leave. It doesn't crystallize into a plan with steps and dates and phone calls that could be made if she wanted relief from the uncertainty. What forms instead is quieter, slower—less instruction than orientation.

Sera feels it as a shift in posture.

The way she stands changes first. Her weight, which has been pitched forward all morning as if preparing to move, settles evenly across both feet. The subtle readiness to bolt loosens. She doesn't sit back down, but she also doesn't scan the beach for an exit the way she usually would.

She simply remains.

The ocean continues its patient work, the tide inching closer with each cycle, testing distance without urgency. The water reaches the place where she stood earlier, smoothing away the last faint outline of her footprints. She watches the erasure without flinching.

For once, she doesn't read it as warning.

She reads it as process.

Her breath deepens without effort. The tightness she's been carrying between her shoulder blades softens, not disappearing, but easing enough to be noticeable. She lifts her shoulders once, rolls them back, then lets her arms hang loosely at her sides.

Her body, finally, is no longer braced against itself.

This is how clarity comes for her—not as resolve, but as alignment. A sense that her internal compass has stopped spinning wildly and begun, at last, to point somewhere consistent.

She knows what she is capable of now.

Not what she will do.

What she can do.

She can stay long enough to be uncomfortable without escaping it. She can remain visible when the instinct to disappear sharpens. She can name the cost of ambivalence without softening it into something more palatable.

She does not yet know if she will choose to pay that cost.

But she sees it clearly for the first time.

The island does not react to this recognition. The dunes remain steady. The horizon stays clean and distant. The wind keeps combing the beach with the same indifferent persistence.

That steadiness feels different now.

Not oppressive.

Honest.

Sera turns back toward the dunes, walking slowly, aware of each step, the way the sand yields and then firms beneath her feet. She traces the path she took earlier, noticing how the light has changed—brighter now, less forgiving. The day has fully arrived.

She does not rush to leave the beach.

She does not linger either.

Movement feels intentional rather than evasive.

At the base of the dunes, she pauses once more and looks back at the water. The line of foam marks the tide's progress, clean and deliberate. She thinks of her father, steady and rooted, choosing presence without guarantee. She thinks of her mother, leaving in order to survive, unwilling to dissolve into a life that no longer fit.

She understands now that both choices were real.

And that refusing to choose has always been one as well.

The knowledge settles without panic.

Without urgency.

She climbs the path back toward the road, hands brushing the rail, fingers tracing grooves worn smooth by years of contact. The wood is warm beneath her touch. Solid. Unremarkable.

Reliable.

The road appears beyond the dunes, empty and waiting. Her car sits where she left it, patient in its ordinariness. She unlocks it but doesn't get in right away, resting one hand on the door, grounding herself in the familiar resistance of metal.

She is aware—keenly—of the absence waiting back at the house. The quiet rooms. The bed that will feel larger tonight. The knowledge that Beckett will not be there, not because he vanished, but because he stepped away with intention.

That absence no longer reads as abandonment.

It reads as consequence.

She exhales, slow and controlled, letting the air leave her lungs completely before drawing it back in. The breath feels earned.

She is not ready to act.

She does not reach for her phone. She does not rehearse a conversation. She does not map out what tomorrow will require.

For once, she allows clarity to exist without demanding it turn into motion.

The island has given her what it offers best—not answers, not comfort, not absolution.

Orientation.

Sera gets into the car and closes the door, the sound firm and final without being dramatic. She sits for a moment longer, hands resting on the steering wheel, gaze fixed ahead.

She knows now what she has been avoiding.

She knows what staying would ask of her.

She knows what leaving would cost.

That knowledge is enough for this moment.

She starts the engine and pulls onto the road, not fleeing, not arriving—simply moving forward with her eyes open, carrying clarity with her like something newly weighted but unmistakably real.

The decision is forming.

She does not touch it yet.

But it is there.

Chapter Ten

The Leaving Place

The apartment is exactly as she left it.

That is the problem.

Sera stands just inside the door, heels still on, keys dangling uselessly from her fingers, and lets the quiet register. Not the coastal quiet of Hatteras—the layered hush of wind and water and distance—but the sealed, interior silence of a building designed to keep the world out.

Charleston hums somewhere below her windows. Traffic. Voices. A siren rising and falling in practiced rhythm. All of it muted by glass and concrete and height.

Her space holds.

Nothing creaks. Nothing shifts in response to her presence.

The air smells faintly of lemon cleaner and whatever detergent the building pipes through its vents. Climate-controlled. Neutral. Safe in the way a showroom is safe—no sharp edges, no evidence of use.

She closes the door behind her and the sound is decisive, cushioned. Final without effort.

The lights come on instantly when she flips the switch. No delay. No flicker. The room fills with an even, flattering brightness that makes everything look intentional. The sofa sits exactly where she positioned it, angled for conversation she rarely hosts. The coffee table is clear except for a single book she never finished. The throw blanket remains folded, untouched.

Nothing here bears witness to urgency.

She sets her bag down and walks through the apartment slowly, as if checking for changes she already knows won't be there. The kitchen counters are bare. The sink is empty. The refrigerator hums quietly, stocked with items chosen for efficiency rather than appetite—yogurt, greens, bottles of sparkling water she always forgets to drink.

She opens the fridge anyway.

The cool air spills out, sterile and contained. She stares at the shelves longer than necessary, then closes the door without taking anything.

Hunger feels irrelevant here.

Her bedroom is worse.

The bed is made too neatly, corners sharp, pillows aligned with architectural precision. The curtains are half drawn, admitting filtered afternoon light that doesn't quite touch the floor. There is no smell of salt. No lingering warmth from another body. Just fabric and order and the faint trace of whatever candle she burned last time she convinced herself to stay in.

She sits on the edge of the bed, careful not to disturb the arrangement, and feels the mattress give slightly beneath her weight before settling back into shape.

Temporary compression.

Immediate recovery.

She presses her palms into the duvet, testing it, then withdraws them, leaving no visible mark.

This place has always prided itself on resilience.

It absorbs her without asking her to adapt.

That used to feel like relief.

She kicks off her heels and lines them up by the door out of habit, toes perfectly even. The gesture feels performative now, like she's continuing a role long after the audience has left.

Her reflection catches her eye in the mirrored closet door.

She looks composed. Put together. The version of herself she cultivated carefully—hair smoothed, posture aligned, expression unreadable but pleasant. This Sera knows how to exist here. She understands the rules. She understands how to succeed without friction.

She looks like someone who belongs.

The realization lands with a dull thud in her chest.

Belonging, she sees now, is not the same as being held.

She stands and moves to the window, pushing it open despite the hum of the air conditioning. The city's warmth presses in immediately, thick and layered with exhaust and food and old stone. The sound swells—voices, engines, movement stacked on movement.

She grips the windowsill, grounding herself in the cool metal.

Below, people move with purpose. Everyone is going somewhere. Everyone has somewhere to be.

She used to love this feeling—the anonymity, the forward motion, the sense that no one was watching closely enough to notice if she changed direction.

No one here would know if she stayed or left.

No one would feel the absence.

The apartment does not argue with her presence or her departure. It does not ask her to choose. It does not care.

That indifference had once felt like freedom.

Now it feels like erasure waiting patiently for her consent.

She crosses back into the living room and sinks onto the sofa, the cushions cool and unmarked. Her body tenses automatically, adjusting itself to furniture that has never learned her shape. She rests her hands in her lap and becomes acutely aware of how little of herself exists in this space.

There are no photographs on the walls. No inherited objects. No things that would require explanation.

She curated safety here.

She curated absence.

The thought comes unbidden and refuses to soften.

She leans forward, elbows on her knees, and exhales slowly, feeling the breath leave her chest in a controlled stream. The apartment remains unchanged. The city continues below. Nothing pushes back.

She understands now why returning felt necessary and insufficient all at once.

This place offers survival without friction.

It offers continuity without consequence.

And in doing so, it asks nothing of her—not her history, not her vulnerability, not her willingness to remain present when staying becomes difficult.

She sits there longer than she intends to, letting the stillness press in from all sides. The silence does not deepen. It does not evolve.

It simply persists.

When she finally stands, it is not because she has reached clarity.

It is because the emptiness has finished making its point.

The apartment does not echo when she moves away.

It never has.

Sera moves through it again, this time with intention, cataloging its refusal to change. Drawers close with the same soft click; counters remain bare; the sink stays cool and unyielding. She remembers the Hatteras pipes' knock, the rust stain—small adjustments the island once required. Here, nothing demands adaptation. She sinks onto the sofa fully this time, closes her eyes, and lets the silence accumulate. Absence, she sees sharply, was never peace. It was insulation: protection from discomfort that also blocked alteration. This place has given her safety without entanglement, a life she can exit without dent. The cost settles in her chest—quiet, certain evidence she has outgrown this shelter.

The apartment has never witnessed her.

Not in the way the island has. Not in the way Beckett did, without trying.

It has not seen her argue with herself. It has not felt the weight of her indecision settle into its bones. It has not shifted or creaked or absorbed her presence in any way that would mark time.

She looks around, suddenly aware of how interchangeable the rooms feel. How easily another life could slide into this space without friction. Another person's furniture. Another person's routines.

Nothing here would protest.

The realization chills her more than the air conditioning ever has.

Work receives her the way it always has: efficiently.

The building smells faintly of coffee and recycled air, the lobby polished to a shine that reflects movement without retaining it. She badges through the turnstile, the soft beep of access approval landing with practiced neutrality. The elevator arrives quickly. Too quickly. No waiting. No small inconvenience to mark the transition from outside to in.

She slides into her chair and wakes her computer. The hum of it feels almost companionable, familiar in its predictability. Notifications populate the corner of the screen, each one a small demand dressed as opportunity.

She answers them in order.

Her fingers know the rhythm. The cadence of professional language returns without effort—measured, precise, reassuring. She reads, responds, edits. She adjusts phrasing to soften edges, to remove any hint of urgency that might be mistaken for need.

Here, urgency is acceptable only when it can be resolved.

She is good at this.

A colleague stops by her desk, leaning lightly against the partition. They discuss timelines. Deliverables. The way a project might shift if one variable changes. The conversation is calm, transactional, efficient.

At one point, he says, "We're glad you're back."

The phrase lands without weight.

She smiles automatically. "Good to be."

And it is—good in the way competence feels good. In the way familiarity eases tension. In the way a system rewards you for understanding its rules.

No one asks where she's been.

No one asks what it cost.

At lunch, she eats at her desk without thinking, unwrapping something chosen for nutrition rather than appetite. The taste barely registers. She scrolls through documents while she chews, eyes flicking back and forth with practiced efficiency.

Her body remains still.

Contained.

This environment does not require her to inhabit herself fully. It asks only that she produce.

She remembers the marina—the smell of fuel and salt, the way sound carried differently over water. She remembers how conversation there unfolded without agenda, shaped by weather and timing rather than calendars.

Here, everything is scheduled.

Predictable.

Safe.

She answers another email and notices, distantly, the absence of sensation. No tightening in her chest. No lift of anticipation. No resistance. The work slides through her like water through a channel already carved.

She has always admired that about herself.

Now, it unsettles her.

The afternoon stretches on, punctuated by soft chimes and quiet footfalls. She edits a document three times until it says exactly what it needs to say and nothing more. She closes it with satisfaction that feels complete but thin.

Her phone sits face-down beside her keyboard.

She doesn't turn it over.

She doesn't need to.

Nothing from the island would intrude here unless she invited it. The walls, the glass, the layers of professionalism—all of it insulates her from anything unplanned.

She leans back slightly in her chair, eyes lifting to the ceiling where recessed lights glow evenly, without flicker. The hum of the building feels constant, dependable. There is comfort in knowing nothing will shift unexpectedly.

She thinks of Beckett's hands, steady on wood, adjusting to grain that could never be fully predicted. She thinks of how the island required attention, how it punished assumption.

This place rewards it.

The contrast sharpens quietly.

Here, she is valued for clarity without vulnerability. For decisiveness without exposure. For staying productive without staying present in any way that might complicate the system.

She realizes, suddenly, how much of her adult life has been shaped by environments like this—spaces that applaud self-sufficiency while gently discouraging entanglement.

She has called that success.

She closes her eyes for a brief moment, then opens them again, returning to the screen. The work waits, patient and exacting. It will take whatever she gives it and ask for more in return.

What it will never ask for is her history.

Her hesitation.

Her willingness to stay when staying means something other than output.

By late afternoon, she has completed everything on her list. She logs off without ceremony, shuts down the computer, gathers her things. No one notices her leaving. No one needs to.

Outside, the city moves around her, busy and unconcerned.

She stands for a moment on the sidewalk, bag on her shoulder, and understands with a clarity that does not demand action—only acknowledgment—that this place has never asked her who she is when she is not useful.

It has only ever asked her to continue.

And for the first time, that is not enough.

She waits until night to open the journal.

Not because it feels ceremonial, but because daylight makes it easier to avoid the parts of herself that go quiet only when the city finally settles. The apartment is dim now, lit by a single lamp she leaves on more out of habit than need. Outside, Charleston hums less insistently, the sounds thinning into something almost gentle.

She retrieves the journal from the bottom drawer of her dresser, where she placed it months ago and then refused to touch. The leather cover is worn soft, corners rounded, the spine cracked in a way that suggests frequent use rather than neglect. It smells faintly of paper and age and something else—cedar, maybe, or salt trapped long ago between pages.

She sits at the small dining table, the journal resting un-opened beneath her hands.

Her fingers hesitate.

This is not curiosity. It is respect. Or fear. Or the recognition that once she reads what is written here, she will no longer be able to imagine her mother's leaving as an abstraction. It will become textured. Specific. Human.

She opens it anyway.

The first pages are mundane—lists, half-sentences, notes that seem written more to anchor thought than to record it. Tide times. Groceries. A reminder to fix the screen door. The ordinariness of it tightens something in Sera's chest. Her mother's life did not begin in crisis. It was lived in details.

She turns the pages slowly, careful not to rush. The handwriting shifts over time—sometimes tight and slanted, sometimes looser, almost drifting. Margins are used freely. Lines cross back over themselves. The journal was not meant for anyone else.

She reads without judgment, letting the voice emerge on its own terms.

There are passages about the island—the way the sound looks at dusk, the way storms feel when they settle rather than rage. There are observations about Sera as a child, written with tenderness but also distance, as if her mother were already practicing how to watch from afar.

Then the tone changes.

Not abruptly. Gradually.

Entries grow shorter. Less descriptive. More inward. Her mother writes about restlessness without naming its cause. About the feeling of being observed by a place that expects something in return. About loving deeply and still feeling hollowed by it.

One passage stops Sera entirely.

I am afraid that if I stay, I will disappear so completely that even I won't remember who I was before.

Sera reads it twice.

Then again.

The words land not as accusation or justification, but as confession. They are not dramatic. They do not ask for forgiveness. They simply exist.

She exhales slowly, the sound loud in the quiet apartment.

Another entry follows, dated only days later.

Leaving feels cruel. Staying feels like surrender. I don't know which version of myself survives either choice.

Sera presses her thumb into the page, feeling the slight give of the paper beneath her skin. She has written versions of this sentence in her head a hundred times without realizing where it came from.

She keeps reading.

Her mother does not portray herself as brave. She does not frame her leaving as liberation. She writes instead about necessity—about the narrowing of breath, about the fear of becoming resentful of the very people she loves.

I am afraid of what I will become if I don't go.

That sentence sits alone on the page, underlined once, the ink pressed harder there.

Sera feels the familiar tightening behind her ribs, the place where understanding gathers before it becomes painful.

Her mother did not leave to be free.

She left to remain intact.

The distinction shifts something fundamental in Sera's thinking.

She flips ahead, then back, then forward again, reading out of order now, guided by instinct rather than chronology. She finds the final entry easily—it is shorter than the rest, the handwriting steadier, almost resolved.

I hope one day she understands that love is not always enough to make a life livable.

Sera closes the journal carefully, as if the pages might bruise if she isn't gentle.

She sits back in her chair, eyes unfocused, the city's distant sounds seeping in around her. Her throat feels tight, but no tears come. This is not grief. It is alignment.

She understands now that her mother's leaving was not a failure of love.

It was an act of self-preservation undertaken too late to spare anyone else the cost.

And her father's staying—she sees it more clearly too—was not passive endurance, but a different kind of sacrifice. One that asked him to absorb loss without dissolving.

Both choices required something to be given up.

Sera has spent her life trying to find a third option.

One where no one pays.

She looks around the apartment again, this time with the journal's weight still present in her hands. The furniture. The quiet. The careful insulation. The version of survival she built for herself here.

It has kept her from disappearing.

But it has also kept her from being fully seen.

The realization does not explode. It settles.

Survival, she understands now, is not the same as living.

Her mother survived by leaving.

Her father lived by staying.

Sera closes her eyes and lets that truth exist without rushing to resolve it. The journal rests heavy and real in her lap, no longer an artifact but a mirror.

She does not know yet what she will do with this understanding.

But she knows—finally—that avoiding disappearance is not the same thing as choosing presence.

And that difference matters more than she has ever allowed herself to admit.

The journal makes it impossible to ignore: she has organized herself around fear of disappearance. Cities of many, jobs of output, relationships of intensity without duration—independence enviable outside, defensible within. She told herself she was building a life; really, she was ensuring she could leave it intact.

The apartment proves how well she learned the lesson: furniture holds no imprint, walls collect no memory, space receives and releases without resistance. She has survived beautifully. She has also remained untouched—disappearing in plain sight, mistaking composure for wholeness, movement for agency, provisionality for safety.

Beckett's back at the marina surfaces—not abandonment, but refusal to disappear. Love without commitment keeps you provisional; provisional lives thin you out. What frightened her most was not loss, but the demand to choose presence over escape.

The binary fractures: stay and disappear, leave and survive. Neither path clean, neither safe. Survival is baseline—the floor, not ceiling. Living is staying visible, shaped, claimed.

The decision arrives not with urgency but stillness. Internal argument falls quiet; shoulders lower, vigilance loosens. Return no longer means retreat but recognition—stepping toward a self who risks being altered. Not choosing Beckett as axis, but returning to herself in a place that notices arrival, demands adjustment, refuses quiet erasure. Freedom without claim is another narrowing.

Fear remains—watchful, not vetoing. There was never a choice without cost. She accepts it now.

She rises, stands in the apartment's center. The decision is inside her, settled, private. No announcement, no debate. That is how she knows it is real.

She does not pack everything.

That is the first decision she notices herself making.

Sera stands in the bedroom with the closet door open, the city's night air drifting in through a cracked window, and lets her gaze move over the orderly rows of clothing. Everything here has a purpose. Everything has been chosen for efficiency, for versatility, for the ability to leave without friction.

She reaches for a hanger, then stops.

Packing everything would turn this into closure. A declaration. A performance she is not ready to give—not to anyone else, and not even to herself.

Instead, she chooses selectively.

She pulls down a soft sweater she hasn't worn in years, one she bought on a whim because it reminded her of salt air and never quite fit into the life she built here. She folds it carefully, pressing the fabric flat with her palms, feeling the faint resistance of wool beneath her hands.

She adds jeans worn thin at the knees. A pair of boots that still carry dust in their seams from a place she didn't mean to miss. A notebook with blank pages that have waited patiently for intention.

She leaves the rest.

The work dresses stay on their hangers. The heels remain lined up by the door. The clean geometry of her city life remains intact, undisturbed. She is not dismantling anything.

She is preparing.

The suitcase slides out from under the bed with a soft scrape. It is smaller than the one she arrived with. She notes that without commentary. She opens it and arranges the items inside with care—not haste, not avoidance. Each piece placed deliberately, as if she is teaching herself how to move forward without erasure.

In the bathroom, she pauses over her toiletries. She leaves behind what can be replaced. She keeps what feels personal—small, almost irrational choices that make sense only to her. A worn brush. A bottle of lotion nearly empty. Things that hold memory in their repetition.

She does not check ferry schedules.

She does not book anything.

This is not logistics yet.

This is orientation.

She moves through the apartment one last time, not to say goodbye, but to notice. The way the light pools on the floor near the window. The silence that does not answer her presence. The absence of resistance in every surface.

She has lived here well.

She has lived here safely.

She sets the suitcase by the door, then stops herself from zipping it closed. The open mouth of it feels right—unfinalized, honest. She places her keys on top, then moves them slightly, then leaves them where they land.

Her phone remains face-down on the counter.

She does not pick it up.

This decision does not require witnesses.

She sits on the edge of the bed, hands resting loosely on her thighs, and breathes. The inhale comes steady. The exhale longer. She feels the difference in her body immediately—the way intention settles when it is no longer being negotiated.

She thinks of Hatteras without romanticizing it.

The wind that never quite stops. The way the house creaks and shifts. The way the island does not accommodate hesitation. She thinks of the space Beckett left—not as rejection, but as integrity.

She understands now that returning is not a promise.

It is a willingness.

To be seen. To be altered. To stay long enough for the shape of her life to register somewhere beyond herself.

She stands and switches off the bedroom light. The apartment darkens evenly, without protest. She leaves the lamp on in the living room, the soft glow familiar and contained.

For a moment, she stands there with her suitcase by the door, the city murmuring outside, the life she built holding its shape behind her.

She does not feel torn.

She feels aligned.

The fear is still there—quiet, observant—but it no longer dictates her movement. It has been folded into the decision rather than allowed to veto it.

She understands that this choice will cost her something.

That has become part of its honesty.

She moves to the window one last time and looks out over the city lights. The view is beautiful in its own way—dense, alive, indifferent. She does not resent it. She does not cling to it.

She lowers the window and turns away.

When she finally reaches for her phone, she does not unlock it. She simply holds it for a moment, feeling its weight, then sets it down again.

Not yet.

This remains hers.

She zips the suitcase halfway and stops, fingers resting on the metal pull. The sound of the zipper hanging unfinished feels deliberate, precise.

The decision is complete.

No announcement. No rehearsal. No need for validation.

She stands in the quiet apartment, surrounded by the life that once defined her, and lets herself acknowledge the truth without ceremony or escape.

She is going back.

Not to reclaim something lost.

But to choose what she has been avoiding all along.

Chapter Eleven

The Return

The ferry smells like diesel and salt and sun-warmed paint.

Sera stands at the rail with both hands wrapped around the metal, knuckles pale where she grips too tightly. The wind off the sound presses damply against her face, lifting stray strands of hair and pushing them into her mouth until she tucks them behind her ear with a quick, impatient motion.

The water below is not the ocean's blue.

It's a shifting green-brown, alive with silt and light, the surface chopped into small, restless waves that slap the hull in steady rhythm. Laughing gulls track the boat for a while, wingbeats slow and deliberate, before peeling away toward a distant line of marsh.

She watches them disappear and feels something in her chest unclench.

Not relief.

Orientation.

The anxiety doesn't arrive as panic.

That's what surprises her most.

Sera has lived with panic before—sharp, immediate, the kind that floods the body and demands flight. This is different. This sits lower, steadier. It hums beneath her skin like an engine left running, a vibration she feels more than hears.

She stands on the ferry deck and lets the wind press against her, salt-stung and insistent, as if it's testing her balance. Her stomach tightens with each small lurch of the boat. She shifts her weight, adjusts without thinking. The motion feels familiar in her bones.

Anxiety, she realizes, is what happens when you try to move and stay still at the same time.

She's not trying to stay still anymore.

The thought lands quietly, without triumph. It doesn't erase the nerves winding through her chest, doesn't slow the tightness at the back of her throat. But it gives those sensations context.

Direction.

She watches the water break against the hull—white foam collapsing back into green-brown churn—and thinks about how many times she's mistaken certainty for recklessness, how often she's trusted fear because it felt intelligent. Charleston taught her that composure could pass for control, that distance could masquerade as wisdom.

Hatteras never let her forget otherwise.

Here, the body knows before the mind does. The weather announces itself hours before it arrives. The tide changes without apology. Staying aware isn't optional—it's survival.

Her fingers curl around the rail, then loosen.

She tests herself in small ways, the way she always has when standing at the edge of something that matters. She asks the old questions first, out of habit.

What if he doesn't believe me?

What if I say it wrong?

What if certainty evaporates the second I speak it out loud?

The questions arrive automatically, practiced and sharp. She lets them pass through her without answering. They no longer feel like warnings. They feel like echoes.

Beneath them, there is something else.

A steadiness she doesn't recognize at first because it doesn't announce itself. It doesn't demand reassurance or proof. It simply exists, quiet and unyielding, like the line of dunes ahead that holds fast against wind and tide year after year without ever claiming permanence.

This is what choosing feels like, she thinks. Not clarity without fear—but clarity that can hold fear without collapsing.

She closes her eyes briefly, the ferry's vibration rising through the soles of her shoes, and imagines stepping off onto the dock. Imagines seeing Beckett's face not as a question mark but as a fixed point. The image doesn't spike her pulse. It steadies it.

That's how she knows.

Anxiety sharpens her senses—every sound too loud, every movement magnified. Certainty narrows them. It strips the moment down to what matters.

Right now, what matters is not how this conversation ends.

It's that she has chosen to have it. The ferry slows, engine pitch dropping, and the crowd shifts with collective awareness. She opens her eyes and watches the island draw closer, the low line of land resolving into scrub and pilings and sun-faded structures that look as though they've been holding their breath since the last storm.

She exhales slowly.

Anxiety tells her all the ways this could fracture—how easily hope can be mistaken for promise, how saying I'm staying does not guarantee permanence. Anxiety reminds her that choice does not inoculate against loss.

Certainty does not argue.

It doesn't counter with assurances. It doesn't claim safety.

It simply says: This is the direction you're facing now.

When she drives off the ferry and onto the road, the sensation follows her. The landscape rushes by—sea oats bending, clapboard houses raised on stilts, hand-painted signs weathered into near-illegibility. Everything looks exactly as it did when she left and entirely different because she is the one moving through it now.

Her hands grip the steering wheel too tightly. She notices and adjusts, rolling her shoulders once, deliberately. The gesture feels almost ceremonial.

You're allowed to be nervous, she tells herself. You're not allowed to pretend that nervousness means you don't know what you're doing.

That distinction feels new.

She thinks of all the times she has waited for certainty to arrive fully formed, believing she needed to feel calm before acting. She thinks of the years she spent mistaking emotional vigilance for responsibility, mistaking hesitation for depth.

Charleston rewarded that version of her.

The island never did.

As she drives toward the marina, anxiety flares again—quick, bright. Her mouth goes dry. Her pulse jumps. She imagines Beckett looking up and seeing hesitation on her face, misreading nerves as doubt.

The thought stings.

But it doesn't derail her.

Certainty steps in—not as confidence, but as acceptance. She cannot control how he receives this. She can only control whether she shows up fully, without retreat.

That's the choice. Her foot stays steady on the gas.

When she pulls into the gravel lot, the sound of tires crunching feels too loud, too final. She cuts the engine and sits there for a moment, hands resting on the wheel, feeling the echo of movement settle into stillness.

This is the moment anxiety would usually take over.

This is where she would catalog exits, rehearse contingencies, prepare to soften the impact of her own desire.

She doesn't.

She opens the car door.

Heat wraps around her immediately, thick and real. The marina noise rises—voices, gulls, the slap of halyards against masts. Life going on, unbothered by the fact that she is about to redraw the shape of her own.

Her legs feel steady as she stands.

That's how she knows, finally, the difference.

Anxiety makes the body brace.

Certainty lets it move.

She closes the door, the sound sharp and definitive, and starts toward the docks—not fearless, not calm, but aligned.

Whatever happens next, she will not disappear from it.

And that, she realizes, has always been the point.

Her sandals clap softly against sun-warmed boards as she moves along the dock. The planks flex faintly under her weight. The water below glints harshly, sunlight splintering into sharp lines.

Halfway down, she sees him.

Beckett is bent over an engine bay, forearms braced, hands deep in grease and metal. He wears a faded shirt with the sleeves pushed up, and his hair is wind-tossed, damp at the edges as if he's been in and out of the heat and spray all morning.

He doesn't look up right away.

And something in that—his focus, his self-contained steadiness—makes her chest ache.

Not with longing.

With recognition.

This is who he has been while she was gone: rooted, working, refusing to drift.

Sera slows but doesn't stop.

Her heart thuds hard enough she feels it in her throat.

Beckett shifts, reaching for a wrench, and the movement changes the angle of his body just enough that he catches her presence in the periphery.

He stills.

Then he looks up.

The space between them goes taut. His expression doesn't soften into relief. It doesn't harden into anger. It becomes unreadable in the way people get when they're holding themselves still to prevent hope from rushing in too fast.

"Sera," he says.

Just her name.

No question.

No accusation.

She stops a few feet away, close enough to smell the salt on him, the sharp bite of engine oil, the sun-warmed clean of his skin. Close enough to see the slight tension at the corner of his mouth.

She doesn't apologize.

Not because she has none to offer, but because she knows apology would make this about the past. And she is not here to reopen what already broke.

She is here to choose.

"I'm not here to ask you to wait," she says, voice steady despite the shake in her hands. She curls her fingers into her palms to hide it. "I'm here to tell you I'm staying."

He blinks once. Slowly.

The muscles in his jaw jump, then still. His hands—still dirty, still inside the engine bay—pause as if he's afraid to move too quickly, afraid motion might shatter what he heard.

"Say that again," he says quietly.

Not demanding.

Needing.

Sera takes one step closer.

"I turned down Charleston," she says. "Not because you asked me to. Not because I'm trying to prove anything. Because I finally understand what I was doing—how I kept surviving by leaving pieces of myself behind."

His gaze holds hers like an anchor.

"I don't know what forever looks like," she continues, throat tightening on the word. "But I know what running looks like. And I'm done."

Beckett stands slowly, wiping his hands on a rag that only smears the grease further. He doesn't come all the way to her. He stops just short, leaving a sliver of space like he's giving her one last chance to step back.

His eyes search her face—not for passion, but for fracture lines. For the places she might still be holding an exit.

"You're here," he says.

"Yes."

"And you're not going to disappear the second it gets hard?"

The question is quiet. It lands like truth.

Sera swallows and forces herself not to soften it with promises she can't guarantee.

"I can't promise I'll never be scared," she says. "But I can promise I won't leave without telling you. I won't make you wake up to absence again."

Something shifts in him then—small but seismic. His shoulders ease. His breath leaves his chest in a slow, controlled exhale, as if he's been holding it since the day she drove away years ago.

He steps closer.

He lifts his hand, hesitates—then lets his knuckles brush lightly against her wrist.

Not possession.

Confirmation.

"You're choosing," he says, voice rougher now.

"Yes," she whispers. "I'm choosing."

He looks at her for a long beat, as if memorizing the sight of her saying it out loud.

"Staying how," he asks.

The question isn't sharp.

It's careful.

A man who has learned the cost of assuming.

Sera takes a breath.

She feels it expand low in her lungs, grounding her.

This is not a declaration meant to sweep them both into relief. It's an agreement she is offering in full daylight.

"Here," she says.

"On the island. In this life. Not as a pause. Not as something I try on."

She watches his jaw tighten, then release.

"I turned down Charleston," she continues.

"I didn't counter. I didn't ask for time. I said no."

His eyes flicker at that—not surprise exactly, but recalibration. As if a weight he's been bracing for has shifted unexpectedly.

"Why?" he asks.

The question matters.

She knows that.

She doesn't answer it with romance.

"Because I finally understood what I was doing," she says.

"I told myself I left to survive. But what I was really doing was disappearing slowly, in places that rewarded distance."

She gestures vaguely toward the water, the boats, the horizon that has never pretended to be anything other than itself.

"This place never let me do that," she adds. "Neither did you."

The admission lands between them, unadorned. She feels exposed in a way that has nothing to do with vulnerability for its own sake. This is exposure as accountability.

"I'm not promising certainty. I'm promising presence." The word feels solid in her mouth.

Presence.

Beckett shifts his weight, the dock responding with a soft creak. He glances once at the water, then back at her, as if orienting himself to a world that has subtly changed shape.

"You're not saying this because you think it'll fix what broke," he says.

"No."

"You're not saying it because you're afraid of losing me."

She considers that, honestly. Then shakes her head. "I'm saying it because I'm afraid of losing myself," she says. "And I finally know that staying—choosing—doesn't mean giving up who I am. It means claiming it."

His breath leaves him in a slow exhale, the sound barely audible over the marina's hum. He rubs a hand over the back of his neck, a gesture that looks more like grounding than hesitation.

"This isn't a grand gesture," he says quietly.

"No," she agrees. "It's a direction."

Silence stretches again, but this time it feels different—less like suspension, more like alignment.

She watches him absorb the words, watches the careful way he lets himself believe without rushing into relief.

"I need to know something," he says finally.

"Okay."

"If this gets hard—and it will—you're not going to disappear."

The statement is flat, factual. Not an accusation. A boundary.

Sera nods once. Firmly.

"I won't," she says. "If I get scared, I'll stay in the conversation. I won't leave you alone with it."

His eyes search hers again, deeper this time, as if looking for the seams where resolve might fray. She holds his gaze without flinching. This is the part she used to avoid—the sustained looking, the refusal to look away when things matter.

"Say it again," he asks. "Not about Charleston. About me."

She steps closer. The space between them narrows until the heat of him feels undeniable, until the dock's gentle sway becomes shared movement.

"I choose you," she says.

The words land differently than I'm staying. More personal. More dangerous.

"And I choose this," she adds. "Not because it's easy. Because it's true."

For a long moment, he doesn't move.

Then he nods—once, sharp and decisive, as if something inside him has locked into place.

"Okay," he says.

Just that.

But the word carries weight. Acceptance. Commitment. The quiet gravity of someone who understands exactly what's being offered and has decided to meet it.

He reaches for her then, not pulling her in but resting his hand lightly at her waist, a touch that asks rather than claims. She leans into it without hesitation.

"This is real," he says.

"Yes."

"And you're here."

"Yes."

The marina continues around them, unchanged. Boats rock gently against their lines. Gulls wheel overhead. Somewhere, a radio shifts songs.

But between them, something has been spoken clearly enough to hold.

Her choice is no longer abstract.

It has a shape now.

And it stands between them, solid and shared.

He doesn't step into her certainty right away.

That, Sera realizes, is the clearest sign of how much it costs him.

Beckett stays where he is, hand still resting lightly at her waist, as if grounding himself through the contact without letting it become proof too quickly. His thumb presses once, almost absentmindedly, then stills. She feels the restraint in it—the deliberate choice not to pull her closer, not to let relief rush in unchecked.

"I hear you," he says slowly. "I just need to be sure I'm not hearing what I want."

The words land with quiet force. Not doubt, exactly. Memory.

Sera nods. She doesn't interrupt. She lets him take the space he needs, even as the part of her that once would have rushed to reassure holds still.

Beckett looks past her for a moment, gaze drifting toward the water, the horizon fractured by masts and rigging. The marina noise seems to recede around him, like he's stepping inward rather than away.

"I've been here before," he says. "Not like this. But close enough to know the difference matters."

Her chest tightens, but she stays quiet. This is his story to speak.

"When you left last time," he continues, voice even, almost too controlled, "you said you needed air. Space. You said it wasn't about me."

She remembers. The words sting because they were true and insufficient all at once.

"I believed you," he says. "But belief didn't change the ending."

He turns back to her then, eyes steady, unflinching.

"So when you say you're staying, I need to know what happens when staying stops feeling like clarity and starts feeling like work."

The question is not hypothetical.

It's muscle memory.

Sera feels the instinct to promise—to say always, to say no matter what—but she stops herself. She knows now that what he's asking for isn't reassurance. It's honesty that can survive erosion.

"I don't know what I'll feel on the hardest day," she says carefully. "I know what I'll do."

He waits.

"I'll talk," she continues. "I'll stay present in the fear instead of pretending it means I need to leave. I won't turn uncertainty into an exit."

Beckett studies her face, as if mapping these words against the woman he has known—the girl who once ran barefoot down these docks, the woman who left without looking back, the one standing here now with her feet planted and her voice steady.

"Say it again," he says.

Not because he didn't hear her.

Because repetition matters to him. Because consistency is the language he trusts.

"I won't disappear," she says. "Not emotionally. Not physically. If I'm struggling, you'll know. You won't have to guess."

His breath catches—just slightly. He looks down at his hand where it rests against her, flexes his fingers once as if testing reality.

"You're not asking me to hold you here," he says. "You're asking me to stand with you."

"Yes."

Another silence stretches between them, but this one feels like recalibration rather than distance. Beckett nods slowly, the movement almost imperceptible.

"I need you to understand something," he says. "I don't need certainty. I've lived on this island long enough to know better than that."

A faint, humorless curve touches his mouth.

"But I do need to know that when the tide shifts—and it always does—I'm not the only one holding the line."

Sera steps closer, closing the last intentional gap between them. She lifts her hand and places it over his, where it rests at her waist. The contact is warm, grounding.

"You won't be," she says.

He watches their hands together, the way her fingers settle without hesitation. The dock sways gently beneath them, a reminder that stability here has never meant stillness.

"You're choosing this knowing it could hurt," he says.

"Yes."

"And you're not asking me to protect you from that."

"No."

His jaw tightens, then eases. The carefulness doesn't vanish, but it changes shape. It becomes something like resolve.

"Okay," he says again, quieter this time.

He lifts his hand from her waist—not withdrawing, but resetting—and then brings both hands up to frame her face, thumbs resting lightly along her jaw. The touch is deliberate, reverent, as if he's asking permission even now.

"This isn't me taking you at your word because I want to believe," he says. "This is me believing because you stayed long enough to say it clearly."

She swallows. "I'm here."

"I know," he replies. "I just needed to hear it without the storm around us."

He leans in then, resting his forehead against hers, their breath mingling.

The kiss doesn't rush to meet her.

It waits.

Beckett stays close enough that she can feel the warmth of him, the steady presence of his breath, the faint brush of his shirt against her wrist where their hands still rest together. The marina sways beneath them, subtle and constant, as if reminding them both that balance here has always been something you choose moment by moment.

He studies her face again—not searching now, but confirming. As if this is the last place doubt could hide, and he wants to be certain it's gone.

Sera feels the familiar pull of anticipation, but it's different than before. It isn't hunger sharpened by absence. It isn't urgency. It's a quiet readiness, the kind that comes when the body and the mind finally stop arguing about what they want.

Beckett leans in slowly.

He gives her time.

Enough time to pull back if she needs to. Enough time to reconsider. Enough time to recognize that this moment isn't being carried by momentum or memory, but by deliberate choice.

She doesn't move away.

Instead, she lifts her chin a fraction, the smallest signal, and feels the answer ripple through her chest like relief.

His mouth meets hers gently at first—not claiming, not testing, just resting there. The contact is warm and steady, a point of connection rather than ignition. She exhales into it, her breath slipping between them, and feels the way his body responds—not by tightening, but by settling.

The kiss deepens, slowly, in increments so small they feel intentional. He angles his head, just enough. She follows without thinking, her hand sliding from his wrist to his chest, palm flattening over the solid beat beneath his shirt.

This is what intention feels like, she realizes.

Not intensity.

Presence.

The marina noise fades—not because it disappears, but because it loses relevance. The slap of water against hulls becomes a rhythm rather than a distraction. Voices blur into background texture. The gulls overhead wheel and cry without urgency.

Everything unnecessary falls away.

Beckett's hand moves from her face to the back of her neck, fingers warm, grounding. The touch is firm but not possessive, anchoring without pulling. She feels the restraint in it—the conscious choice not to take more than what's being offered.

She answers by leaning in, not pressing, not asking for escalation, just aligning herself with him fully. Their bodies fit together naturally, as if they've been practicing this kind of closeness all along without knowing it.

The kiss lingers.

It's unhurried in a way that feels almost radical. No rush toward more. No need to prove anything. Just the sustained truth of contact, of being here together without an exit in mind.

When Beckett finally pulls back, it's by inches, their foreheads still touching, their noses brushing lightly. He doesn't open his eyes right away. Neither does she.

They breathe.

In. Out.

Together.

"This isn't a pause," he says quietly, voice low against her mouth.

"No," she agrees. Her voice doesn't shake.

"This isn't something we borrow from time."

"No."

His thumb traces a small, absent circle at the base of her neck, then stills. She feels the weight of the gesture—the way he's grounding himself as much as her.

"This is us choosing," he says.

"Yes."

The word feels different now that it's been lived into, not just spoken.

He opens his eyes. She does too.

The look they share isn't charged with drama. It's calm. Clear. Almost startling in its simplicity. The fear that once sat between them—always unnamed, always bristling—has been acknowledged and allowed to settle. It hasn't vanished. It has been integrated.

Beckett rests his forehead against hers again, just briefly, as if sealing the moment without ceremony.

"I'm not waiting anymore," he says.

Sera feels the truth of that statement like a quiet shift in the ground beneath her feet. Not pressure. Not demand.

Alignment.

"Neither am I," she replies.

He steps back then—but only half a step, enough to look at her fully, to see her standing here without retreat, without armor. His hands remain on her arms, thumbs resting lightly where her pulse beats steady.

"This will take work," he says.

"I know."

"And patience."

"Yes."

"And honesty, even when it's uncomfortable."

She nods. "Especially then."

A small smile touches his mouth—not triumphant, not relieved. Just real.

"Okay," he says. "Then we're doing this."

The simplicity of it lands with weight.

They don't kiss again right away. They stand there for a moment longer, hands still linked, letting the choice settle into their bodies. Letting the marina witness it without fanfare.

Sera becomes aware of the heat again, the salt in the air, the steady rocking beneath them. The island hasn't changed in response. It doesn't need to.

This choice isn't about spectacle.

It's about direction.

Beckett squeezes her hand once—gentle, deliberate—and releases it, not in withdrawal but in trust. She doesn't reach for him immediately. She lets the space exist, lets it hold the shape of what they've just claimed.

When she does step closer again, it's without urgency.

Without fear.

They turn together toward the dock, toward the boats, toward the life waiting in plain sight. Nothing has been erased. Nothing has been promised beyond what they can carry honestly.

But something essential has shifted.

They are no longer waiting.

They are choosing.

Together.

Chapter Twelve

The Storm That Stays

The rain begins without urgency.

Sera notices it first as a soft change in the air, a cooling that slips across her skin like a held breath finally released. The sky has been low all afternoon, clouds pressed flat and heavy, but the light never sharpened into warning. No sudden wind. No violent shift. Just the sense that something patient had decided to arrive.

She stands at the window and watches the first drops darken the deck boards, each one blooming into the grain of the wood before disappearing into it. The sound follows—a quiet, steady tapping that spreads across the house until it becomes a rhythm rather than a disruption.

This is not a storm that demands attention.

It doesn't rattle the windows or push at the doors. It doesn't flash or announce itself. It settles. Claims the evening gently, as if the island itself has decided to soften.

Sera exhales without realizing she's been holding the breath.

Rain like this always felt different on Hatteras. Less like weather, more like a presence. As a child, she used to sit on the porch steps during these slow showers, counting the seconds between drops that slid off the eaves, convinced she could feel the island breathing beneath her feet. Her father would tell her not to get soaked, his voice carrying from inside, but he never insisted too hard. He understood the difference between danger and communion.

This rain carries that same understanding.

She presses her palm lightly against the glass. It's cool there, faintly vibrating with the quiet insistence of water meeting wood. The smell follows soon after—salt dampened, earth drawn up from the marsh, the faint metallic tang of rain hitting old nails and railings. The house absorbs it all without complaint.

Behind her, Beckett moves through the room without sound. She doesn't turn right away. She can feel him there—presence without pressure, a steadiness that no longer spikes her awareness but deepens it.

The rain grows more consistent, smoothing into a near-constant hush. It blurs the edges of the yard, softens the line between deck and dune. The island looks gentler like this, less exposed. As if it has chosen to pull a thin veil over itself and rest.

"This one's going to last," Beckett says quietly, from somewhere near the kitchen.

Sera nods, though he can't see her. "Yeah."

He doesn't say more. He doesn't need to. The rain has already said it for him. This is not the kind that breaks things apart. This is the kind that settles in for the night.

She turns then, leaning back against the window frame, and watches him move—slow, unhurried. He rinses his hands at the sink, water running low and steady, fingers working methodically to remove the last traces of the day. The simple domesticity of it catches her off guard. Not because it's new, but because it no longer feels provisional.

Outside, the rain thickens slightly, enough to be heard clearly now on the roof, on the tin edge of the shed, on the tops of the railings. Each surface answers differently. The house becomes a map of sound.

She remembers storms that demanded vigilance—nights spent awake, counting seconds between thunder, measuring risk. This rain asks nothing of her. It doesn't test. It doesn't threaten.

It stays.

Sera crosses the room and sits at the table, resting her hands flat against the worn surface. The wood is smooth under her palms, softened by decades of use. She traces a shallow groove with her thumb, one her father carved absentmindedly while working out a problem years ago. The house holds those marks openly. It never tried to erase what shaped it.

The rain doesn't ask the island to prove itself, she thinks.

It trusts the ground to take it in.

Beckett joins her without ceremony, setting two mugs down between them. The steam rises briefly before dissolving into the cooler air. He sits across from her, posture relaxed, gaze steady.

The rain continues its quiet work.

Sera listens to it, lets it fill the spaces where her mind used to rush ahead. She realizes, with a small shock, that she is not bracing for anything. Not for loss. Not for the moment when calm gives way to consequence.

This rain isn't a pause before something worse.

It's an arrival in its own right.

The sound wraps the house in a way that feels almost protective. It blurs the edges of time, smoothing the sharp distinctions between then and now. The island feels less like a proving ground and more like a held space.

She thinks of all the times she mistook intensity for meaning, urgency for depth. Of how storms once felt like mirrors for her own chaos—proof that love had to arrive with force to be real.

This rain tells a different story.

It says: endurance doesn't have to be loud.

Beckett lifts his mug, pauses, then sets it back down untouched, eyes flicking briefly toward the window before returning to her. His expression is open in a way that still surprises her—unguarded, present.

"Feels different," he says.

She knows what he means. Not just the rain. Everything.

"It does," she agrees.

The house creaks softly as the temperature shifts, wood adjusting to moisture the way it always has. The sound feels companionable now, familiar rather than foreboding.

Outside, the island lets the rain fall without resistance.

Inside, Sera feels something settle into place—not as certainty, but as safety. The kind that doesn't depend on holding everything still. The kind that allows movement without fear.

The rain keeps coming, steady and calm.

And for the first time in longer than she can remember, she doesn't wait for it to stop.

They move through the evening without ceremony.

That's what strikes Sera most—the absence of performance. No one announces transitions. No one asks what comes next. The rain keeps its steady rhythm outside, and inside the house they fall into motion the way people do when they trust the space to hold them.

Beckett dries the mugs and sets them upside down on a towel, careful not to let them clink. The sound feels too sharp for the quiet they've settled into. Sera watches his hands as he works—not with the charged awareness that once made her breath hitch, but with a softer attention. She notices the way he checks the rim of each cup with his thumb, the way he aligns them without thinking, as if order itself is a kindness.

She clears the counter, wiping down a spot that isn't really dirty. The cloth smells faintly of lemon oil and old cotton. She moves slowly, deliberately, giving the moment weight by refusing to rush through it. The house seems to approve—no sudden creaks, no protesting hinges. Just the low, companionable sounds of wood and rain.

They don't talk much.

When they do, it's about small things. A loose board on the back step that needs fixing. The way the tide's been running higher than usual in the afternoons. Whether the shrimp boat that came in earlier belonged to the Evans family or someone new.

Ordinary observations. Shared attention.

Sera realizes how long it's been since she's allowed herself this kind of closeness—the kind that doesn't require intensity to justify its existence. In other places, intimacy always felt like a negotiation. Here, it's a rhythm.

Beckett moves to the old radio by the window and adjusts the dial until a low, crackling blues station settles into place. The music is distant, imperfect, threaded with static. He turns the volume down until it's barely there, more texture than sound.

"That okay?" he asks.

She nods. "Yeah."

He doesn't ask why. He doesn't fill the silence with explanation. He simply accepts the answer and lets the music do its quiet work.

Sera sits at the table and folds a stack of clean dish towels she found in the drawer, smoothing each one before stacking it neatly. It's a small, almost absurdly domestic task, and she feels a flicker of emotion she can't quite name move through her chest. Not grief. Not joy.

Recognition.

This is what staying looks like when no one is watching.

Beckett joins her a moment later, pulling out the chair beside hers instead of across from her. Their shoulders brush lightly as he sits. The contact is unremarkable and grounding at the same time. She doesn't tense. He doesn't pull away. They simply adjust until the fit feels natural.

He reaches for one of the towels and folds it again—not correcting her, just participating. Their hands work in parallel, occasionally bumping, then separating. Each small collision feels like a quiet acknowledgment rather than a spark.

Outside, the rain deepens slightly, the sound shifting as it hits different surfaces. The house responds with a soft sigh of settling, beams adjusting to the damp air.

"Hungry?" he asks after a while.

"A little."

He stands and opens the fridge, peering inside with mild skepticism. "Options are limited."

"Limited is fine," she says.

He smiles faintly at that, over his shoulder, then sets to work with what's available—bread, cheese, the last of the tomatoes from the counter. He slices slowly, deliberately, the knife making a soft, steady sound against the cutting board.

Sera watches from the table, chin propped on her hand. The sight of him doing this—feeding them without making it a point—loosens something inside her. She thinks of all the meals she's eaten alone in pristine kitchens, the silence there polished and hollow.

Here, the quiet has texture.

He sets the plates down between them without comment and sits back beside her. They eat without hurry, the rain and music filling the space around their small, shared sounds. She tastes salt and tomato and bread warmed just enough to soften. Simple. Enough.

Halfway through, Beckett reaches for her plate without looking. "Let me," he says, and wipes a smear of juice from the edge she missed.

The gesture is so casual it nearly slips past her. Nearly.

She stills, breath catching just slightly, then lets it go. This, too, is intimacy. Care without spectacle. Attention without demand.

"Thanks," she says.

He nods, as if it's nothing. As if this is what people do when they're not afraid of what care might cost them.

Afterward, they stand at the sink together, shoulders nearly touching as they rinse the plates. She hands him one; he takes it. The choreography is imperfect, occasionally awkward, but they don't comment on it. They adapt.

When they finish, he turns off the light over the sink and the room dims, the rain-lit windows becoming the primary source of glow. The house feels smaller, warmer.

They don't reach for each other right away.

Instead, they sit on the couch, close but not pressed together, legs angled toward each other, the space between them intentional and easy. Sera tucks her feet beneath her, the fabric of the cushion cool against her ankles.

Beckett rests his forearm along the back of the couch, not touching her, just there. The proximity is enough.

Outside, the rain keeps falling, steady and untroubled.

Inside, Sera feels the unfamiliar comfort of a night that doesn't ask her to prove anything. No urgency. No performance. Just the quiet, enduring act of sharing space.

And for the first time, that feels like more than enough.

The honesty arrives without drama.

It doesn't announce itself the way it used to—no sharp intake of breath, no bracing for impact. It settles between them gradually, carried in on the quiet of the rain and the way the house seems to exhale around their stillness.

They sit on the couch, angled toward each other but not touching, the small space between them intentional rather than guarded. The radio murmurs softly from the corner, the blues threaded with static, and outside the rain keeps its steady rhythm against the roof. The sound makes everything else feel less exposed, as if the house has agreed to hold what's said here.

Sera watches her hands resting in her lap. She notices the faint tremor in her fingers—not fear exactly, but the residue of habit. For so long, honesty felt like something that had to be negotiated, softened, prepared for. It always came with a cost she tried to calculate in advance.

Now, the cost feels different.

"What are you thinking?" Beckett asks.

His voice is low, unforced. Not a prompt. An invitation.

She doesn't answer right away. She lets the question settle, lets herself feel where the truth lives before she gives it shape.

"That this feels... easier than I expected," she says finally. "And that part of me doesn't trust that."

He nods, unsurprised. "Fair."

She glances at him, a small smile flickering and fading. "I'm used to things feeling earned. Hard. If it's calm, I assume I'm missing something."

Beckett shifts slightly, turning more fully toward her. The couch cushion dips with the movement, the proximity increasing without pressure.

"I used to think that too," he says. "That if something didn't cost me, it wasn't real."

She meets his gaze, sees the truth there without defensiveness. The openness steadies her.

"And?" she asks.

"And I got tired," he says simply. "Not of wanting. Of bracing."

The word lands softly but precisely.

Sera exhales. The sound feels like a release she didn't realize she'd been holding back.

"I've been afraid of what happens when I stop bracing," she admits. "Like if I relax into something, I'll lose the right to leave if it goes wrong."

Beckett considers that, his expression thoughtful rather than reactive. "What if leaving isn't the only way to protect yourself?"

The question is gentle. It doesn't push.

Sera looks down again, tracing the seam of her jeans with her thumb. The rain shifts outside, deepening for a moment before settling back into its steady cadence.

"I don't know how to stay without disappearing," she says quietly. "I've done it both ways. Left to survive. Stayed and shrank."

He doesn't interrupt. He waits.

"I'm afraid that if I stay fully," she continues, "I'll wake up one day and realize I've made myself smaller again. That I traded one kind of loss for another."

The admission feels risky—not because it will provoke anger, but because it names something she has always tried to outrun.

Beckett nods slowly. "That makes sense."

No correction. No reassurance.

Just recognition.

"I don't want you to disappear either," he adds. "Not into leaving. Not into staying."

She looks at him then, really looks. The lines at the corners of his eyes, the way his mouth rests when he's not guarding his words. There is no expectation in his gaze. No demand that she be anything other than what she is right now.

"What do you do with that fear?" she asks.

He thinks for a moment. Outside, the rain taps against the window frame, a soft punctuation.

"I don't make it a decision-maker," he says. "I let it exist. I tell it what's happening, instead of letting it decide what I do."

The simplicity of it surprises her.

"I've been letting fear run the whole operation," she admits. "Calling it practicality."

A faint smile touches his mouth. "Fear's good at rebranding."

She laughs softly, the sound brief and genuine. It feels like a crack in something old and rigid.

They sit with that for a while, the rain and radio filling the spaces where they don't rush to speak. Sera feels the unfamiliar ease of saying something true and not immediately preparing for its consequences.

"I need you to know something," she says after a moment.

He turns fully toward her now, attention complete.

"If I pull back sometimes," she says, choosing each word carefully, "it won't be because I'm leaving. It'll be because I'm learning how to stay without armor."

Beckett's breath leaves him slowly. He nods once. "I can work with that."

"And if you need space," she adds, "I won't read it as rejection."

"I'll tell you when I do," he says. "And when I don't."

The clarity of it settles into her chest like warmth.

She shifts closer without thinking, their shoulders touching lightly. The contact feels natural, uncharged. He doesn't tense. He doesn't move away.

"This feels like we're telling the truth without trying to solve it," she says.

"Yeah," he agrees. "Feels like that."

Outside, the rain continues, steady and patient. The island holds the house without testing it, the way it sometimes does after storms. Inside, Sera feels the unfamiliar safety of honesty that doesn't demand resolution.

Not everything is settled.

Not everything is known.

But for the first time, truth feels like something she can live inside without fear.

Beckett doesn't name his vulnerability outright.

It arrives sideways, in the way he stands at the counter rinsing two mugs that are already clean, in the carefulness of his movements, as if the quiet might shatter if he moves too fast. Sera watches him from the table, chin resting on her hand, noticing things she once would have missed—the slight hitch in his breath when he thinks she isn't looking, the way his shoulders loosen only after he finishes a task, not before.

This is not the Beckett who met storms head-on.

This is the Beckett who stays when the weather no longer requires heroics.

She realizes, with a small ache behind her ribs, that she has spent years interpreting his steadiness as invulnerability. As if rootedness meant immunity. As if the man who never chased could not be afraid of being left behind.

"Hey," she says softly.

He turns, mug in hand. "Hey."

There's a question in his eyes he doesn't voice. She recognizes it now—the habit of waiting for permission even when none is required.

"You don't have to keep moving," she says. "You can sit."

He hesitates. Just a fraction. Then he sets the mug down and crosses the room, lowering himself into the chair across from her. The table between them feels deliberate, not distancing. A place to rest their hands. A place to be seen.

Sera studies the grain of the wood beneath her fingers, worn smooth by decades of use. Her father's table. The surface holds dents and scratches that never weakened it.

"I've been thinking," she begins, then stops. Reroutes. "No. I've been noticing."

Beckett's mouth curves slightly. "That sounds more danger-ous."

She huffs a quiet breath. "You're allowed to be scared, you know."

The smile fades, replaced by something more careful. "I know."

"But you don't let yourself be," she says. Not an accusation. An observation.

He looks down at his hands—broad, capable, marked by old cuts that never fully faded. He turns them palm up, as if weighing the truth there.

"I don't trust fear," he says after a moment. "It tells you to grab things too tight. Or not at all."

"That's still fear deciding," she says gently.

He meets her gaze, something unguarded flickering there. "I figured if I kept my footing steady, I could take the hit when it came."

The words land heavier than she expects.

"When," she repeats.

A muscle in his jaw tightens. "Storms don't ask permission."

Neither do departures.

She feels the recognition settle between them—how differ-ently they learned the same lesson. She learned to run before the impact. He learned to brace and hold.

"I didn't know how much you were risking by staying still," she says.

He exhales slowly. "I didn't either. Not until you came back."

The admission is quiet, but it opens something.

Sera shifts her chair back just enough to step around the table. She doesn't rush. She doesn't close the distance all at once. When she reaches him, she rests her hand lightly on his forearm, giving him time to pull away if he needs to.

He doesn't.

His skin is warm beneath her palm. Solid. Real.

"You've been carrying this like it's yours alone," she says. "Like wanting me was something you had to manage instead of something we could name together."

Beckett swallows. His gaze drops to where her hand rests, then lifts again. "Wanting something that might leave feels reckless."

"Wanting something that might leave is human," she replies.

For a long moment, neither of them speaks. The rain taps steadily against the windows, the sound less like pressure now and more like accompaniment.

"I was afraid," he says finally, the words barely above the rain, "that if I admitted how much it mattered, I'd lose the part of me that knows how to stand."

Sera's chest tightens. "You don't lose that by letting me see it."

He considers that, the idea turning slowly in him. "You don't disappear by staying," he says, testing the shape of it. "And I don't collapse by hoping."

She nods. "That's what I'm learning too."

She slides into the chair beside him, close enough that their knees touch. The contact is grounding, not electric. She leans her head briefly against his shoulder, a small gesture weighted with intention.

"You don't have to be unafraid to be with me," she says. "You just have to let me know where the fear lives."

His arm comes around her, tentative at first, then settling. The hold is not protective. It's present.

"I'm afraid of waking up and finding the house quiet again," he admits. "Of learning how to breathe around your absence."

Sera closes her eyes, absorbing the honesty without trying to fix it. "I'm here," she says. Not a promise. A fact.

He nods against her hair, his breath evening out as if the truth itself has steadied him.

The rain continues outside, unhurried. The island holds its shape. Inside, Sera recognizes the depth of what he's offered—not certainty, not guarantees, but the courage to be seen in the wanting.

And she knows, with a clarity that feels earned, that acknowledging his vulnerability doesn't make him less solid.

It makes him real.

And real, she is finally ready to stay with.

Her fear doesn't disappear.

That's the first thing Sera understands as she sits there with Beckett's arm warm around her shoulders, the rain steady against the house. It hasn't been erased by choice or soothed into obedience by love. It still lives in her body, alert and watchful, the way it always has.

But it feels different now.

Smaller, somehow. Or maybe not smaller—contained. Like water held by banks instead of flooding everything in reach.

She lets herself notice it without flinching. The tightness that comes when she imagines a future with edges she can't see. The old instinct to scan for exits, to calculate what she would lose if she stayed too long in any one place, with any one person. Fear has always spoken to her in the language of preparation.

Don't get trapped.

Don't owe anyone more than you can carry.

Don't make a choice you can't undo.

For years, she listened to those warnings as if they were wisdom.

Now, sitting here in the softened light of the living room, she hears something else underneath them.

Fear isn't asking her to leave.

It's asking her to stay alert.

The realization comes quietly, without the drama she once expected from transformation. She has always thought fear was a verdict—final, authoritative, something to obey or escape. But what if it's only information? A signal that something matters enough to risk?

She shifts slightly, adjusting against Beckett's side. He tightens his arm reflexively, then relaxes again, as if reminding himself that holding her doesn't require vigilance anymore. The small movement grounds her.

"I've been thinking about fear wrong," she says.

He hums softly, encouraging her to continue without interruption.

"I thought it meant I was about to lose something," she says. "Or that I was making a mistake."

"And now?" he asks.

"And now I think it just means I'm close to something real."

The words surprise her with their simplicity. She waits for her chest to tighten, for the familiar recoil. It doesn't come.

Instead, there's a sense of alignment—like a joint easing into its natural position after years of strain.

Fear, she realizes, was never the problem.

Avoidance was.

She has spent so much of her life treating fear as a stop sign that she never learned how to read it as a landmark. Something that said: here. This matters. Pay attention.

The rain shifts outside, growing slightly heavier for a moment, then settling back into its steady rhythm. The house absorbs the sound without complaint. Nothing rattles. Nothing threatens to come undone.

"I used to think staying meant giving something up," she says. "That if I chose one life, I'd have to abandon all the other versions of myself."

Beckett's thumb traces a slow, absent line along her arm, the touch grounding rather than distracting. "And now?"

"And now I think leaving was how I avoided integrating them," she says. "I kept myself intact by never letting anything fully take hold."

The admission lands with weight. She feels it in her throat, her chest. Not shame. Recognition.

Fear, reframed, becomes something like a compass needle. It doesn't dictate direction, but it tells you when you're facing something powerful enough to change you.

She tilts her head slightly, resting it more fully against Beckett's shoulder. The contact feels earned—not a refuge, but a partnership in stillness.

"I'm still afraid," she says quietly. "Of losing you. Of losing myself. Of waking up one day and realizing I made a choice I can't reverse."

He doesn't rush to reassure her. He doesn't offer platitudes or promises. He simply lets the truth exist between them.

"Yeah," he says. "That makes sense."

The lack of resistance in his response is what changes everything.

Her fear doesn't need to be argued with. It doesn't need to be conquered. It needs to be allowed into the room without being handed the keys.

She exhales slowly, feeling the difference between being ruled by fear and being accompanied by it.

"I don't want to make decisions anymore just to quiet it," she says. "I want to make decisions that can hold it."

Beckett nods, his chin brushing lightly against her hair. "That's the kind of fear you can live with."

She thinks of the island—how it never promises safety, only continuity. How storms come and go, how erosion reshapes the shoreline inch by inch without destroying the land entirely. The island doesn't eliminate risk. It accommodates it. Builds around it. Lives in conversation with it.

She understands now that love here works the same way.

Not as a shelter that keeps fear out, but as a structure strong enough to withstand its presence.

"I always thought permanence meant stillness," she says. "Like once you chose something, you had to freeze around it."

Beckett's arm tightens briefly, then settles. "Permanence is just choosing to adjust instead of escape."

The words settle into her like truth she's been circling for years.

Her fear shifts again—not gone, not silenced, but recalibrated. It no longer points her toward exits. It points her toward care. Toward honesty. Toward the ongoing work of staying awake inside a life instead of skimming its edges.

She feels a quiet gratitude for that fear now—not for the pain it caused, but for what it reveals. That this matters. That she is risking something real. That she is alive to the stakes instead of numbing herself to them.

Outside, the rain continues its patient fall.

Inside, Sera lets herself understand, fully and without retreat, that fear does not disqualify her from love.

It confirms that she is finally brave enough to remain inside it.

The island does not ask anything of them that night.

The rain keeps its even pace, soft enough that the sound blends into the house rather than challenging it. The wind moves through the sea oats without snapping them. The sound stays calm, its surface dark and steady beyond the windows. The island feels less like a proving ground and more like a basin—something wide enough to hold whatever is placed inside it.

She looks around the room—the lamp throwing a soft halo against the wall, the couch bearing the imprint of where they sit, the table holding the small evidence of their evening without commentary. Everything feels anchored. Not frozen. Anchored.

"This place isn't pushing tonight," she says softly, more to herself than to Beckett.

He glances toward the window, then back at her. "It does that sometimes."

She nods. "I forgot."

Or maybe she never learned to recognize it before. She was always bracing, always reading pressure as meaning. She didn't know how to interpret gentleness without suspicion.

The island, she realizes, is not testing them because it doesn't need to.

They have already crossed the threshold it demands.

She feels it in her body—the absence of vigilance. The way her shoulders have lowered without her instructing them to. The way her breath deepens naturally, unguarded. This is not the stillness of waiting for impact. It's the stillness of something allowed to rest.

She thinks of the times she mistook intensity for approval. Of how she read storms as signs—warnings or permissions—when really they were just weather, indifferent to her interpretations. The island was never asking her to endure more. It was asking her to pay attention.

Now, paying attention means noticing what isn't happening.

No tension in the floorboards.

No whine of wind probing the seams.

No sharp edges demanding response.

She shifts slightly, and the house responds with a soft creak, the sound companionable rather than alerting. The island doesn't flinch at their movement. It accommodates it.

"It feels like we're being... allowed," she says, the word tentative but accurate.

Beckett hums softly, an agreement without elaboration.

Allowed.

She turns that over. She has spent years thinking permission had to be earned through struggle. That if something didn't resist her, it couldn't be trusted. But here, the island offers something simpler and more difficult to accept: welcome without conditions.

The island holds their quiet without amplifying it. It does not ask them to prove their choice with drama or endurance. It lets their decision exist as something ordinary and therefore durable.

Sera closes her eyes briefly, letting the steadiness register.

For the first time, she understands that belonging here was never about surviving the storm.

It was about knowing when the island had decided to stop testing—and learning to trust the shelter that follows.

This, she understands, is what it feels like when love stops demanding proof. When it no longer needs to be chased or secured or accelerated into something undeniable. When it trusts itself enough to remain quiet.

She feels safe not because nothing can hurt her, but because nothing is trying to rush her toward an answer.

The island holds the night steady around them. The house shelters without enclosing. The rain finishes what it came to do and fades.

Sera leans into Beckett's side, and he adjusts without thought, his arm coming around her with an ease that feels practiced and new all at once. They do not speak. They do not move toward the bedroom. They do not mark the moment as significant.

They let it be ordinary.

And in that ordinariness, she recognizes something she has never fully trusted before: a love that doesn't need urgency to survive.

A love that makes room.

A love that feels, finally, like safety inside love.

Chapter Thirteen

The Choice That Remains

Dawn arrives without ceremony.

Not the kind that announces itself in color or drama, but the quieter version Hatteras favors after weather—light thinning the dark by degrees, the horizon easing into visibility as if it's careful not to wake anyone too abruptly. Sera opens her eyes to that in-between state where night hasn't fully released its hold and morning hasn't yet claimed the room.

The house is still.

Not the brittle stillness that follows damage, but a settled one. Wood cooling after humidity. Air rearranging itself. The faint, familiar scent of salt and damp pine lingering in the corners.

She doesn't move right away.

Beckett is warm beside her, the weight of him known before she consciously registers it. His arm lies across her waist with an ease that suggests sleep didn't loosen it. His breathing is slow, even, the kind that belongs to someone who no longer expects interruption.

Outside, the sound rests.

She listens for it—the water, the wind, the low conversation between island and weather—and finds it balanced. The tide has turned sometime in the night. She can tell by the way the sound has shifted farther out, less insistent against the shore. The wind has rotated west, softer now, carrying warmth instead of edge. Sea oats whisper instead of rattle.

After the storm, the island has chosen continuity.

Sera lets that register before she lets anything else in.

She shifts slightly, testing the moment the way she used to test departures. Beckett's hand tightens, then loosens, settling again at her waist. The movement is instinctive, unguarded. He doesn't wake. He doesn't search.

The closeness feels assumed.

That's new.

For so long, every morning carried a question—Are you still here? Did something change while I slept?—as if the night might quietly revise the rules. She'd learned to wake with a kind of vigilance, her body already half-prepared for loss or recalculation.

This morning holds no such edge.

She notices it in the way her breath stays low. In the absence of the familiar inventory she used to take—distance, options, contingencies. There's no internal rush to define or secure what this is before it slips away.

It doesn't feel provisional.

Light creeps farther into the room, catching on the worn dresser, the soft curve of Beckett's shoulder, the edge of the window frame where salt has dulled the paint. The house looks inhabited rather than paused, as if it's already adjusted to their presence without commentary.

Sera studies the small details: the faint scar at Beckett's collarbone she's traced before, the way his hair curls at the nape of his neck when the air is damp, the crease in the pillow where his head rests. These are not discoveries. They're confirmations.

She has known this body in fragments—nights, moments, returns—but never like this, stitched into morning without urgency.

She closes her eyes again, just briefly, and lets the understanding settle.

This feels different now.

Not because something grand has changed overnight, but because nothing is asking her to leave. Not the island. Not the house. Not the man beside her.

She listens to the sounds of the morning taking shape. A gull somewhere inland. The distant hum of an early truck on the road. The subtle creak of the house as temperature shifts. These are not disruptions. They're markers of a life continuing.

Beckett stirs then, a small sound at the back of his throat, his breath changing rhythm. His arm tightens again, more deliberately this time. She feels his awareness arrive before his eyes open.

"Morning," he says quietly, voice still rough with sleep.

"Morning."

Neither of them moves.

They lie there in the widening light, the moment unclaimed and unhurried. Beckett's thumb traces a small, absent circle at her waist, not a question, not a request. Just contact.

"How's the weather?" he asks, eyes still closed.

She smiles faintly. "It's decided to behave."

He hums, something like agreement. "Figures."

She tilts her head slightly, resting her forehead against his shoulder. The position feels natural, practiced, as if her body has always known where it belongs and simply waited for permission to remember.

Outside, the wind moves through the marsh grass in long, even strokes. No sharp gusts. No warnings. The tide continues its slow withdrawal, leaving darkened sand behind, patient and altered but intact.

Sera thinks of all the mornings she woke with plans already forming around escape—how to leave without hurting anyone, how to stay without disappearing. She recognizes now how exhausting that constant negotiation was, how it narrowed her life into exits and strategies.

This morning asks nothing of her.

It doesn't demand decisions or declarations. It doesn't require proof. It simply offers itself and waits to be lived.

Beckett opens his eyes and looks at her, his expression clear, unburdened by questions he once would have carried. There is no searching in his gaze. No bracing. Just presence.

"Coffee later?" he asks.

"Yeah," she says. "Later."

The word lands with weight—not delay, but permission. There is time. There will be time.

He presses a brief kiss to her hair, not to claim the moment, not to mark it as significant. Just because she's there.

Sera exhales, a long, quiet breath she didn't realize she'd been holding for years.

The storm has passed.

Not in the way storms usually do here—no debris to catalog, no repairs demanding attention. Just a gentle recalibration. The island has shifted back into its rhythms, and she has shifted with it.

She understands now that permanence doesn't arrive as certainty.

It arrives as mornings like this.

Still. Ordinary. Undeniably real.

And for the first time, that is enough.

Morning makes a practice of them.

Not the dramatic kind—no declarations, no pause heavy enough to announce itself—but the quiet, ordinary sequence of motions that settle into place as if they've been rehearsed for years. Sera wakes to the sound of Beckett moving through the kitchen, the soft clink of a mug against the counter, the scrape of a chair leg eased carefully back so it won't shriek across the floor. The house breathes around these sounds, accepts them.

She doesn't rush to join him.

That, too, feels new.

When she does rise, she pulls on yesterday's shirt without thinking and pads down the narrow hall. The floorboards give under her feet in familiar complaint. Light spills in from the east-facing window, pale and steady, turning the dust in the air into something almost deliberate. Beckett stands at the counter, back to her, pouring water into the kettle with the unhurried attention of someone who knows the weight of it by heart.

"Morning," he says, without turning.

"Morning."

It lands easily between them.

She moves past him to the sink, rinses her hands, reaches for a mug from the open shelf. The mug is chipped at the rim; she chooses it anyway. He notices, not because it matters, but because noticing has become part of the rhythm. He slides the honey closer without comment. She takes it, leaves a small ring of stickiness on the counter, wipes it away with the heel of her palm.

This is what it looks like, she thinks, when nothing needs to be proved.

They eat standing up, leaning against opposite counters, trading pieces of toast like currency. Butter melts too fast in the warmth. Coffee steams and then doesn't. The rain from the night before has left the air clean and open, the windows cracked just enough to let the breeze thread through. It lifts the corner of the curtain, drops it again.

After breakfast, there are things to do. Not important things. Small ones.

A loose hinge on the back door. A pile of driftwood that needs moving before it attracts ants. The coil of rope by the shed that's been sitting too long in the sun. Beckett heads outside without announcing it, and Sera follows, not because she's asked to, but because she knows where he's going.

She hands him the screwdriver when he reaches back for it. Their fingers brush—brief, unremarkable. No spark. No pause. The absence of both feels like a gift.

"You don't have to," he says, nodding toward the rope.

"I want to," she replies, already bending to lift it.

The work is simple and physical. She feels it in her arms, the steady pull and give of the rope as they coil it together. The fibers are rough against her palms. Salt dusts her skin. Beckett works beside her, not watching, not directing. When the coil slips, he steadies it with his knee. When she misjudges the length, he adjusts without comment.

They fall into step.

Later, she sweeps sand from the porch while he oils the hinge. The broom makes a soft whispering sound, back and forth, back and forth. He tests the door, opens and closes it until it moves easily, then wipes his hands on a rag that has seen better days. She notices how he folds it afterward, careful, habitual. He notices how she leaves the broom propped against the railing instead of returning it to the hook.

Neither of them remarks on it.

There is a moment, passing, when her shoulder brushes his as they cross paths. He steadies her by the elbow, automatically, and lets go just as automatically. The touch is functional, assumed. It doesn't ask for anything else.

Sera feels something settle in her chest.

She has spent years thinking love would announce itself every time it appeared—that it would require recognition, negotiation, a kind of constant awareness. This feels different. This feels like the opposite of vigilance. Like trust being allowed to rest.

Inside again, she washes the breakfast dishes while Beckett sorts through a box of old nails and screws, choosing what can be saved. The water runs warm over her hands. The smell of soap mixes with salt and oil and the faint sweetness of coffee grounds. He hums, barely audible, a tune she doesn't recognize and doesn't ask about.

She dries the last plate and sets it in the cabinet. When she turns, he's leaning against the table, watching her—not with the intensity that once made her feel seen and exposed, but with something gentler. As if he's memorizing the way she moves now, the ease of it.

"You're good at this," he says, and she knows he doesn't mean the dishes.

"So are you," she replies.

It's not a compliment traded like currency. It's an observation. It sits between them, complete.

They take the coffee mugs out to the porch and sit side by side on the steps. The yard is damp and green, the marsh beyond it quiet in the low morning tide. A heron lifts itself from the water and settles again farther down, patient. The wind has shifted since dawn, coming from the south now, warmer, carrying the faint sound of surf.

Sera leans back on her hands, stretches her legs out into the sun. Beckett does the same. Their knees touch. Neither of them moves away.

She realizes, with a small, steady clarity, that she is no longer measuring this moment against what it might cost her later. She isn't cataloging exits. She isn't rehearsing explanations. The thought feels almost foreign.

Belonging, she understands, doesn't announce itself with certainty. It arrives quietly, disguised as routine.

When Beckett stands, he offers her his hand without looking. She takes it. The gesture is easy, unremarked. He helps her up, releases her, then pauses.

"Want to walk down to the shed?" he asks.

"Sure."

They move off together, their steps falling into rhythm without effort. The house behind them looks occupied now—not waiting, not braced, just used. The island doesn't feel like it's watching them anymore. It feels like it's gone back to its own business.

As they walk, their hands brush once more, then settle together, fingers loosely linked. No spark. No jolt. Just warmth, and the steady knowledge of another body moving alongside her.

Sera breathes in, slow and deep.

This, she thinks, is how love learns to last.

The fear doesn't arrive loudly.

It doesn't knock or demand attention. It waits until the afternoon has softened, until the small tasks are done and the day has lost its edges, and then it settles between them like a tide that has come in without being noticed.

They are inside, the house open to the breeze, windows lifted, doors unlatched. Light slants through the front room, catching on the grain of the floor, the worn arm of the couch, the stack of mail Beckett hasn't sorted yet. Sera sits at the table with a glass of water, watching condensation gather and slip down the sides. Beckett leans against the counter, arms folded loosely, his posture unguarded.

It feels safe enough to speak.

That's what startles her—the absence of urgency. The fact that nothing is breaking. That nothing has forced the moment.

"I'm still afraid," she says.

The words land quietly. She doesn't dress them up. Doesn't soften them. She keeps her voice level, almost conversational, because the fear itself isn't sharp right now. It's familiar. Old. Patient.

Beckett doesn't interrupt. He shifts his weight slightly, the floorboard answering with a low creak, and waits. His eyes stay on her face, not searching, not braced.

"Not of you," she adds, because it matters. "And not of this."

She gestures vaguely, the house, the day, the way they've moved together without effort. Her hand stills against the table, fingers curling lightly against the wood as if to anchor the thought.

"I'm afraid of what happens when things stop feeling immediate," she says. "When there isn't a reason to decide quickly. When staying becomes... ordinary."

She expects that word to feel like a diminishment. It doesn't.

Beckett exhales slowly. Not a sigh. Just breath released with intention.

"I get that," he says.

It's not agreement for the sake of peace. It's recognition.

She studies his face, the calm line of his mouth, the way his jaw tightens and then loosens again. This is the version of him that doesn't rush to reassure, that doesn't rush to solve. She realizes how much she trusts it.

"I've made a habit of leaving before things get quiet," she continues. "Before they ask me to show up without an excuse. I tell myself I'm choosing myself, but half the time I'm just... disappearing early."

Saying it out loud costs something. She feels it in the way her chest tightens, the way her shoulders pull inward before she consciously straightens them. She doesn't want to shrink this moment.

Beckett nods once. He rubs a thumb along the edge of the counter, a small, grounding movement.

"My fear runs the other direction," he says.

She waits.

"I'm afraid of wanting something I can't keep," he continues. "Of letting myself hope and then having to pretend I didn't."

There it is. Not dramatic. Not new. Just finally spoken.

"I've spent a long time telling myself that patience is the same thing as strength," he says. "That if I don't ask for more, I won't lose what I have."

He glances toward the window, where the light has shifted again, softer now, less insistent. The island hums outside—wind in the grass, the distant thrum of a boat engine moving slow through the sound.

"But wanting you," he says, turning back to her, "means admitting that waiting isn't neutral. It's a risk."

Sera feels the truth of it settle in her bones. Not heavy. Clear.

"I don't know what the future looks like," she says. "And I don't want to pretend I do."

"I don't either," he replies.

There is no disappointment in his voice. No relief, either. Just honesty held steady.

She stands, moves toward him, then stops a few feet away. The space between them feels deliberate, chosen. She doesn't cross it yet.

"I can't promise certainty," she says. "I can promise presence. I can promise that if I start to pull away, I'll say it out loud instead of vanishing."

Beckett's shoulders ease, just slightly. The change is subtle but unmistakable, like a knot loosening.

"That's all I'm asking for," he says. "Not guarantees. Just... not being left alone with the wondering."

She nods. The word lands cleanly. Wondering. She has lived inside it for years, mistaken it for freedom.

He steps closer then, closing the distance without urgency. He doesn't reach for her immediately. He gives her time to adjust to the nearness, to the heat of his body, the familiar alignment of their heights.

"Hope still scares me," he admits, quieter now. "But it scares me less when I don't have to hold it by myself."

Sera feels something unspool in her chest—not relief exactly, but permission. Permission to stay in the conversation. To let fear exist without giving it the steering wheel.

She reaches out and rests her hand against his forearm. The contact is light, deliberate. He looks down at it, then back at her, and places his other hand over hers. The warmth of it spreads, slow and steady.

They stand like that for a moment, breathing in sync without trying to. The house creaks softly as it settles around them. Outside, the tide shifts again, neither rushing nor retreating.

No promises are made.

No vows offered.

Just two people acknowledging the shape of what remains uncertain—and choosing, for now, not to run from it.

Sera leans her forehead against Beckett's shoulder, the gesture instinctive, unguarded. He rests his cheek against her hair, careful, present.

This, she realizes, is what courage looks like when it isn't loud.

Truth spoken calmly.

And held.

They return to the shoreline without calling it that.

No announcement, no sense of ceremony. Beckett grabs his keys from the hook by the door. Sera slips on her sandals. The afternoon has eased into something gentler, the heat no longer pressing but lingering, like a hand left at the small of her back after a dance has ended.

They drive with the windows down.

The road curves familiar and narrow, flanked by sea oats and scrub pine, the occasional flash of water visible between dunes. The air smells like salt and sun-warmed asphalt. Sera rests her elbow on the window frame, lets the wind slide across her skin. Beckett's hand stays loose on the wheel, his other arm relaxed against the door.

They don't talk much.

They don't need to.

When they park, the beach is nearly empty. A weekday quiet. The tide is on its way in—not rushing, not dragging its feet—just steady, reclaiming what it left behind hours earlier. Wet sand darkens near the waterline, smooth and reflective, the sky faintly mirrored in its surface.

Sera steps out of the car and pauses.

She's been here before. Not just this beach, but this exact stretch of it—the place where the dunes soften and the shoreline curves inward, offering a kind of shelter from the wind. She remembers standing here years ago, toes dug into cold sand, watching the water with the sharp ache of someone who hasn't yet learned how to stay.

Then, the tide had been on its way out.

She hadn't understood the significance at the time. Only later did she realize how much she'd mistaken retreat for clarity.

They walk toward the water now, their steps unhurried. Beckett kicks off his shoes and carries them by the laces. Sera does the same, letting the sand cool the soles of her feet. The grains shift under her weight, give and settle again. She feels the ground respond to her presence, not resisting, not yielding too easily.

The island, she thinks, is not asking anything of her today.

It's simply bearing witness.

They stop where the first thin line of water reaches them, just enough to darken the sand around their feet. The tide slides in, touches, pulls back, repeats. Beckett stands close, not crowding her, but near enough that their arms brush when the breeze shifts.

She watches the water for a long moment.

"I stood here once," she says finally, the words surprising her with their steadiness. "Right after my father got sick. I told myself I was just taking a break."

Beckett doesn't look at her. He keeps his gaze on the horizon, where water and sky blur into one long, breathing line.

"And I knew," she continues, "that if I stayed any longer, I wouldn't leave at all."

She expects regret to surface with the memory. It doesn't. What she feels instead is distance—not coldness, but perspective.

"I thought leaving was the brave thing," she says. "I thought staying would mean giving something up."

Beckett shifts slightly, sand rasping under his heel.

"And now?" he asks.

She turns to him then, meets his eyes. The question isn't a test. It's an opening.

"Now it feels like staying is the only way I don't disappear."

The words land without weight. They don't tremble. She recognizes that as its own kind of resolution.

Beckett nods once. "That makes sense."

No commentary. No argument. Just acceptance offered cleanly.

The tide comes closer, water curling around their feet, cool and insistent. Sera lifts one foot instinctively, then sets it back down, letting the water take its time. Beckett does the same. They stand together, ankles submerged, the ocean making small decisions around them.

She notices how different this feels from before. How her body isn't braced for impact, isn't counting seconds until she has to move again. The horizon no longer looks like an exit. It looks like a companionable distance—something that exists whether or not she chases it.

Beckett reaches for her hand, not urgently, not possessively. His fingers close around hers with quiet certainty. She laces her fingers through his, the fit familiar, comfortable.

"You don't feel like an anchor anymore," she says softly.

He smiles, faint and real. "Good."

"You feel like..." She searches for the word, then lets it go. Some things don't need naming.

They walk a little farther down the beach, still holding hands, still quiet. A pair of gulls circle overhead, arguing about something unimportant. The sound of the surf grows fuller as the tide advances, the rhythm steady and forgiving.

Sera glances back once, just once, at the stretch of shoreline they left behind. The sand already looks different, smoothed and reshaped by water. Footprints fade quickly here. The island does not preserve hesitation.

She turns forward again.

This time, she doesn't feel the urge to measure how far she's come or how far she might go. She doesn't frame the moment as a decision or a turning point. It simply feels complete in itself.

Beckett walks beside her, matching her pace without effort. He is not pulling her forward. He is not holding her back.

The island doesn't ask anything of them as they move together along the waterline.

It receives them.

And for the first time, Sera understands that arrival isn't a single moment—it's a practice.

They return to the house as evening lowers itself gently over the island.

Not with the sense of coming back to something unfinished, but with the quiet acceptance of a place that has already adjusted to their presence. The light has changed again—no longer the clear, revealing brightness of afternoon, but the softened gold that settles into corners and makes even worn things look intentional.

The wind has eased. It moves now in slow passes, lifting the curtain once, then letting it fall. The tide is still coming in, though farther out, its sound reduced to a steady hush that underlines the silence instead of interrupting it.

Sera steps inside first.

The floorboards answer her weight with the same familiar creak, but it feels different now—not like a greeting, not like a warning. Just acknowledgment. The house smells of salt and coffee and the faint trace of oil from Beckett's hands. Lived-in. Used.

Beckett closes the door behind them, not shutting out the world so much as marking the boundary between what's theirs and what isn't required of them anymore. He sets his keys on the hook by the door, an unremarkable gesture that lands with unexpected finality.

There is nowhere else he needs to be tonight.

They move through the rooms without speaking, each falling into small, unclaimed tasks. Sera rinses the last of the sand from her ankles at the sink. Beckett switches on a lamp instead of the overhead light, choosing the softer glow without comment. Shadows stretch and settle along the walls, not hiding anything, just easing the edges.

When she turns from the sink, he's leaning against the counter, watching her—not with the attentiveness of someone afraid the moment will break, but with the ease of someone who trusts it to hold.

She crosses the room and stops in front of him. There is no pause filled with expectation. No question in the space between them. She rests her forehead briefly against his chest, the contact instinctive, grounding. He folds his arms around her, slow and sure, the way you hold something you know isn't going anywhere.

Outside, the horizon darkens. The first stars emerge, faint but steady, not competing with one another for attention. The island exhales into night.

They stand like that for a long moment.

No urgency. No counting.

Sera becomes aware, then, of what is missing.

The restless scanning of exits. The quiet rehearsal of departure. The sense that love is something that must be managed before it manages you.

None of it rises to meet her now.

Instead, there is this: the warmth of another body, the steady cadence of shared breath, the way the house seems to hold the sound of them without echoing it back too loudly.

When they finally move, it is toward the porch.

They carry their mugs outside and sit side by side on the steps, shoulders touching, knees angled comfortably toward one another. The wood beneath them is still warm from the day, grain worn smooth by decades of weather and use. The yard stretches out before them, darkened now, marsh grass whispering softly in the breeze.

The island does not feel like it is watching.

It feels like it has settled.

Sera looks out toward the sound, where the water catches what little light remains and holds it. She thinks, briefly, of all the times she stood at this edge imagining elsewhere—imagining that distance itself could be a kind of solution.

She understands now how narrow that thinking was.

Elsewhere had never been the answer.Neither had escape.

What she needed was the courage to stay present long enough for something to become ordinary.

Beckett shifts beside her, their hands brushing where they rest on the step between them. This time, there is no spark because there is no doubt. He turns his palm upward. She places her hand in it. Their fingers lace together naturally, the fit familiar without being restrictive.

"This feels…" she begins, then stops.

She doesn't need to finish. He nods, as if she has.

"Yeah," he says.

They sit in the quiet until the light is almost gone, until the house behind them glows softly through the windows, until the tide completes its slow work for the evening. Somewhere down the road, a porch light flicks on. A radio plays faintly, then fades.

The world continues.

But it no longer feels like it's moving without her.

Sera leans her head against Beckett's shoulder, not seeking reassurance, not asking for anything beyond what already exists. He rests his cheek against her hair, the contact light and unassuming.

There is no cliffhanger waiting beyond this moment.No unspoken condition.No open door held back "just in case."

The island, the house, the quiet stretch of night—everything seems to agree on the shape of what has been chosen.

Presence.Partnership.The daily, deliberate act of staying.

As the wind moves once more through the marsh and the tide settles into its patient rhythm, Sera understands that permanence does not announce itself with certainty.

It arrives quietly.

And when it does, it does not ask to be chased.

It simply stays.

Afterword

Hatteras Island is a real place with a living history, shaped by weather, work, and generations of people who have learned how to stay. While this novel draws inspiration from the Outer Banks—their geography, rhythms, and coastal culture—the story, characters, and events are fictional.

Specific locations, businesses, and personal histories have been imagined or altered in service of the narrative. Any resemblance to real places or individuals is incidental, not representational. This novel is offered not as documentation, but as interpretation—an emotional landscape shaped by memory, tide, and return.

Thank you for spending time on Hatteras Island.

If this story stayed with you, you are warmly invited to leave a brief review or share the book with someone who might find meaning in it. Readers often discover these novels through quiet recommendation.

For updates on future books in *The Hatteras Island Cycle*, you may also visit the author online.

Your presence here matters more than you know.

Excerpt from What the Tide Keeps

Next book in the Hatteras Island Series

The story continues in
WHAT THE TIDE KEEPS
Book II of
The Hatteras Island Cycle

Continue the Hatteras Island Story

The story of Beckett Crowe and Sera Bennett continues in the next Hatteras Island novel.

Winter is coming to the island.

Work slows.

Water changes.

And some things the tide returns are not meant to stay buried.

The following is an excerpt from:

WHAT THE TIDE KEEPS

Chapter One

Morning arrived thin and pale across the yard.

The tide had dropped overnight, exposing the darker bands of marsh mud along the edge of the sound. The water pulled slowly past them, moving without urgency toward the inlet, leaving narrow rivulets that traced their way through the grass before settling again.

A faint line of foam caught briefly against the reeds before dissolving.

Beckett was already in the bay.

The air inside carried the smell of damp wood and salt pushed inland by the night wind. Light entered through the open doors in a long narrow angle that stretched across the floorboards and stopped just short of the hull.

The hull rested in its cradle where he had left it the evening before. The seam along the midsection had cured enough to sand, though the air still carried enough dampness that he worked slowly, letting the grain guide the pressure rather than forcing it.

The rasp moved along the surface in steady strokes.

Each pull of the tool raised a thin curl of pale dust that drifted down and settled against the concrete floor.

Outside, a gull settled briefly on the fencepost, folding its wings with a sharp shake before lifting again without landing.

Beckett stepped back and ran his palm across the curve.

Smooth.

Not finished.

The salvaged plank from the workbench now held the east rack firmly in place. He noticed it without looking at it directly, the way a carpenter notices the integrity of a room by the way it carries weight.

It had settled overnight without shifting.

The screws held tight against the grain, the old wood accepting its new purpose without complaint.

He returned to the hull.

The rasp moved again.

The yard gate clicked.

He glanced toward the road as Sera stepped through carrying two mugs.

The wind lifted a strand of her hair across her face before she brushed it back with the side of her wrist. The coffee steamed in the cooler air, the smell of it mixing briefly with the sharper scent of resin and sanded wood.

"You've been at it awhile," she said.

"Since light."

She handed him the mug.

The coffee warmed his hands immediately.

They stood beside the hull without speaking, both looking along the curve where the morning light struck the wood. The grain caught the pale light differently in each section—some bands absorbing it, others reflecting it faintly where the sanding had begun to smooth the surface.

"It held," she said after a moment, nodding toward the rack.

He followed her glance.

"Yeah."

"Good."

She took a sip of coffee and turned slightly toward the road.

"You still need hardware for the west brace?"

"Couple lag screws," he said.

"And that hinge."

"Yeah."

She nodded once.

"I can come with you."

He considered the hull, then the sky.

Clouds had begun to move in from the sound, flattening the light and muting the brightness that had briefly touched the yard.

"Alright," he said.

He set the rasp down and wiped his hands on a rag.

Sera stepped outside the bay while he gathered the tools he would leave behind. The wind carried the faint smell of diesel from somewhere down the road, likely from a boat returning to the harbor after the early run.

Beyond the fence, the sound moved quietly through the exposed mud flats, the tide still slipping outward before the turn.

When Beckett stepped outside, Sera was standing near the gate watching the water.

The marsh grass bent under the wind and lifted again, each movement slow and patient.

"You almost finished with that seam?" she asked.

"Couple more passes."

She nodded.

He could tell she was looking at the water more than the yard.

"What is it?" he asked.

She pointed toward the darker bands of mud.

"The tide dropped farther than yesterday."

He glanced toward the shoreline.

"Wind pushed it out."

"Will it come back the same way?"

"Eventually."

She watched it another moment before turning back toward the truck.

The morning held that quiet stretch of time between tides when the water seemed to hesitate before choosing direction again.

Beckett locked the bay doors halfway and followed her.

The yard remained still behind them.

The rack brace held.

The hull waited.

And the sound continued its slow movement toward the inlet, carrying the faint memory of the night wind across its surfaceThe drive into town took less than ten minutes.

The road curved through low stands of scrub pine before opening briefly where the marsh widened along the water. The sound lay flat beneath the low sky, the tide still easing outward along the mudbanks where the reeds grew thin.

A pair of pelicans drifted low over the water before angling toward the harbor.

Sera watched them pass.

Winter had begun emptying the shoreline in small ways. The docks they passed along the road carried fewer boats than they had in summer. Some slips sat empty, their lines tied neatly to cleats as if waiting for vessels that would not return until spring.

A charter boat idled near the harbor mouth, its diesel engine carrying across the water in a slow steady rumble.

Beckett slowed slightly as they approached the bend where the road met the cluster of older buildings near the waterfront.

The hardware store sat near the corner where the town narrowed toward the docks. Its wooden siding had faded unevenly under years of salt and sun, the paint wearing lighter where the afternoon light struck it most often.

The sign above the door creaked once in the wind.

Beckett parked beside a pickup he recognized.

"Porter's truck," he said.

Sera leaned forward slightly to look through the windshield.

The truck bed held two plastic bins and a coil of netting.

"Here for screws?" she asked.

"Probably bait."

She smiled faintly.

They stepped out of the truck.

The wind carried the smell of the harbor immediately—diesel, salt, and the faint metallic scent of wet rigging.

Across the street, two men stood beside a skiff on a trailer tightening straps along the hull. The trailer wheels rested in a shallow puddle left by the previous night's tide.

One of the men glanced up briefly as Beckett and Sera crossed the street, then returned to tightening the strap without comment.

Inside, the store smelled faintly of fertilizer and wood shavings.

Rows of bins lined the center aisle, each labeled in careful black marker. Nails, screws, washers, bolts—sorted by size and weight rather than brand.

The heater hummed quietly near the counter, pushing warm air toward the ceiling where it lingered before drifting back down.

Carla stood behind the register flipping through a catalog.

She looked up as the door closed behind them, the small bell above it chiming once.

"Well," she said. "Look what the tide brought back."

The line carried no sharpness.

Just observation.

Sera stepped forward first.

"Morning, Carla."

Carla came around the counter and hugged her lightly, the way people do when they are not certain whether time has changed the distance between them.

"Been awhile," Carla said.

"Some things take longer," Sera replied.

Carla nodded once, accepting the answer without pressing.

She turned toward Beckett.

"You keeping him in line?" she asked Sera.

Sera glanced at Beckett.

"I'm trying."

Carla smiled.

"Good luck with that."

Beckett moved toward the hardware aisle while they spoke.

The boards under his boots creaked slightly where the floor had settled over the years. He knew exactly where the lag screws were kept.

The bins had not moved in years.

He reached for the size he needed and dropped four into his palm before adding two more. The metal felt cold and slightly oily from the coating that kept the threads from rusting.

He rolled one between his fingers briefly, checking the pitch out of habit before placing them in the small paper scoop hanging beside the bin.

Behind him, Carla's voice carried easily through the store.

"We all figured you were gone for good," she said to Sera.

Sera did not sound defensive.

"I thought so too," she said.

The words landed without weight.

A man at the far end of the aisle glanced briefly in their direction before returning to the shelf he had been examining.

Beckett stood still for a moment longer than necessary before turning back toward the counter.

Carla leaned against it with her arms folded.

"Island's funny that way," she said. "You think you've left it, but it keeps track of you anyway."

Sera smiled slightly.

"I noticed."

Carla looked between the two of them.

"How's the yard holding?" she asked Beckett.

"Fine."

"Storm last week twisted a couple roofs down the road."

"Missed us mostly."

Carla nodded toward the screws in his hand.

"Fixing something?"

"Rack brace."

She rang them up without comment.

The register drawer slid open with its familiar metal click.

Coins shifted as she made change.

"Good to see you back," she said to Sera as she handed over the receipt.

"Good to be here."

Carla looked toward the door where the wind pressed faintly against the glass.

"Well," she said. "Island remembers who belongs to it."

Sera met Beckett's eyes briefly.

He looked away first.

They stepped back outside.

The air had cooled slightly while they were inside.

The harbor had grown busier during the short time they had been in the store. A small trawler moved slowly along the far dock, its engine churning the water into a dull gray wake that spread across the slips.

Gulls circled above it, their calls sharp in the colder air.

Beckett placed the small paper bag of screws on the seat between them before starting the truck.

Neither spoke as they pulled back onto the road.

Behind them the hardware store door swung closed again, the bell chiming faintly before the sound disappeared beneath the steady movement of the harbor wind.

The sound lay flat under the low sky.

They reached the yard just as the tide began turning again.

The change was subtle at first. The water that had been sliding steadily toward the inlet slowed along the mudbanks before shifting direction, drawing back toward the sound in small overlapping currents.

A faint line of foam gathered along the reeds before drifting inward again.

Beckett turned the truck into the gravel drive and cut the engine.

The quiet returned immediately.

Sera stepped out first and walked toward the bay, her boots leaving shallow impressions in the thin sand along the fence line. The wind pressed lightly against her jacket before settling again.

Beckett remained beside the truck for a moment longer.

Across the sound a skiff moved slowly along the far shoreline, its outboard humming faintly as it traced the edge of the marsh channel. The sound carried easily across the flat water.

Carla's words lingered in his mind without attaching themselves to anything specific.

The island remembers.

He shut the door and followed Sera inside.

The bay carried the same quiet it had held when they left.

Dust from the morning sanding had settled along the floor where the light from the open doors caught it in narrow streaks. The hull waited in its cradle, unchanged except for the section he had smoothed earlier.

The rack brace still held.

Nothing had shifted.

But the yard felt slightly different than it had that morning.

Not unstable.

Just observed.

Beckett set the paper bag of lag screws on the bench and opened it without looking inside. The screws slid into his palm with a dry metallic sound.

Sera had already moved toward the hull.

She ran her hand along the midsection where he had been sanding earlier, feeling the curve rather than examining it.

The wood carried the faint warmth of the morning light where it struck the surface.

"Still smooth," she said.

"Not finished."

She nodded.

He crossed the bay to the east rack and checked the salvaged plank from the workbench again. It had not shifted overnight or during the morning's damp air. The wood had taken the weight naturally, settling into the frame as if it had always belonged there.

He placed one hand against the rack and leaned his weight into it briefly.

The brace held without complaint.

He positioned the new board for the west rack.

The board rested unevenly at first until he adjusted the lower edge against the frame.

"Hold that," he said.

Sera stepped forward immediately and braced the lower end with both hands.

Her boots shifted slightly on the floor as she steadied the board.

He aligned the board, checked the angle once with his eye, then drove the first lag screw slowly through the pilot hole.

The drill whirred briefly before the screw bit into the wood.

The grain tightened around the threads as the head sank flush.

He drove the second.

The brace pulled solid against the frame.

He leaned his weight against it once, testing.

Solid.

Sera released her grip and stepped back.

"That'll carry it," he said.

"For now," she replied.

He glanced at her.

She was not challenging him.

Just acknowledging time.

He set the drill aside and returned to the hull.

The rasp moved again across the seam he had repaired two days earlier. The sound of it filled the bay evenly, the same rhythm it had carried for years.

Outside, the wind shifted briefly and pressed against the open doors before moving on across the yard.

Sera moved through the space quietly, gathering the last of the tools from the dismantled workbench legs stacked by the fence. She lifted one of the boards and brushed away the sand that had collected along the grain before setting it aside.

The cloth she used to tie the remaining tools carried the faint smell of oil and old sawdust.

She knotted it once and set the bundle beside the truck bed where the remaining wood waited to be taken to Ray.

The marsh beyond the fence moved in slow waves as the wind crossed the grass.

Neither of them mentioned the conversation at the hardware store.

Beckett worked until the seam felt uniform beneath his hand.

He wiped the dust away and stepped back.

The hull carried the light cleanly again.

Sera stood near the doorway watching the water beyond the yard.

The tide had begun moving inward more clearly now, covering the darker mudbanks that had been exposed earlier that morning.

"You heard what she said," Beckett said finally.

She didn't turn.

"Yes."

He leaned the rasp against the bench.

"She wasn't wrong."

"No."

He studied her profile for a moment.

"You mind it?"

She shook her head slightly.

"People remember what fits their story," she said.

"And yours?"

She turned toward him.

"I came back."

He held her gaze.

"That's enough for me."

The answer landed plainly.

No defense. No explanation.

He nodded once and turned back toward the rack, adjusting the final screw with a small twist of the wrench.

Outside, a truck slowed briefly along the road before continuing past the yard without turning in.

The sound faded quickly.

Sera stepped farther into the yard, her boots pressing into the thin layer of sand along the fence line.

The marsh grass bent with the wind but did not break.

Beckett joined her after a moment.

They stood beside the open gate, looking toward the sound.

The tide had moved another few inches inward since they returned from town. The water slid quietly around the darker bands of mud that had been exposed earlier.

It did not hurry.

It never did.

"Island remembers," he said after a while.

"Yes."

She did not sound bothered by it.

He looked down the shoreline where the marsh curved toward the inlet.

"You ever think about leaving again?"

She did not answer immediately.

The wind moved across the water and flattened its surface briefly before letting it ripple again.

"I think about where I am," she said.

"And?"

"And I'm here."

He watched the water.

"That's not the same thing."

"No," she agreed.

"But it's enough."

He considered the answer the way he might consider a seam that had been sanded smooth but not yet sealed.

Not finished.

But sound.

Behind them, the yard remained quiet.

The salvaged plank from her father's workbench held the east rack steady. The new brace held the west.

The hull waited where it had waited all morning, unchanged except for the small section he had finished smoothing.

The island had not shifted.

It had only noticed.

The wind changed before the sky did.

Beckett noticed it in the yard the way he noticed a seam that had shifted under his palm—subtle at first, then undeniable once you named it.

The air carried a colder edge, the kind that pressed through a jacket rather than around it. The marsh grass leaned in one direction and stayed there longer than it should.

By midmorning, the sound was no longer flat.

Small ripples ran across it in tight lines, moving fast and low, as if something beneath the surface had begun pulling harder than usual.

Inside the house, Sera stood at the kitchen table with the tide chart open, her father's tide log beside it.

Beckett came in from the yard with a coil of rope over his shoulder.

"You feel it?" he asked.

Sera looked up from the chart.

"The wind."

He nodded.

She glanced toward the window.

"It's sharper," she said.

"North," he replied.

She studied the tide chart again.

"High tide tomorrow's later," she said.

"Wind'll push it higher."

She didn't ask how he knew.

She was beginning to trust the way he read water.

Beckett set the rope on the table and reached for the weather radio on the counter.

He turned the dial until the static cleared.

A voice broke through in steady cadence—numbers, directions, warnings delivered without emotion.

"...coastal waters... northeast winds increasing... building seas... gale watch possible..."

He turned the volume down.

Sera watched him.

"You think it's coming?" she asked.

He didn't answer immediately.

Outside, a gust hit the side of the house and moved along it like a hand.

"Yes," he said finally.

Sera nodded once.

"What do we do?"

Beckett glanced toward the yard.

"Same thing," he said. "We tie down. We bring in anything that can go."

She stood without hesitation.

"Tell me what."

He looked at her for a moment.

Not gratitude.

Not surprise.

Just a quiet recognition.

"Start with the porch," he said. "Furniture. Anything loose."

She nodded and moved toward the door.

Beckett picked up the rope and followed.

By noon, the yard had begun to look different.

Not damaged—prepared.

The bay doors were lowered halfway. The smaller skiffs were pulled deeper inside and blocked. Tools that normally lived on open benches had been boxed and moved off the floor.

Sera moved through the space with practical steadiness, lifting what needed lifting, asking only when a decision actually mattered.

"Where do you want these?" she asked, holding two fuel cans by their handles.

"In the shed," Beckett said. "Back corner."

She carried them without comment.

Beckett checked the dock line next.

The small section of pilings behind the yard wasn't large, but it mattered. In heavy wind and surge, anything tied there could pull hard enough to snap hardware or loosen boards.

He crouched and tested the cleat with his hand.

It held, but he didn't like the slight give.

He stood and looked down the dock.

The boards were damp already, slick under the thin gray light.

The sound had darkened.

Sera stepped onto the dock behind him.

"Is it safe?" she asked.

"For now."

She stopped beside him and looked out at the water.

The wind pushed the surface into constant motion.

No stillness anywhere.

Beckett handed her the rope.

"Hold that line," he said, nodding toward a skiff tied off on the outer cleat.

She took it and braced her feet.

He tightened the knot with quick, practiced turns.

The rope pulled taut.

He tested it once.

"Good," he said.

Sera kept her grip until he nodded again.

She let the line settle against the cleat.

"What's it going to do?" she asked.

"The wind'll push water in," Beckett said. "Not all at once. It'll sit high longer than it should. That's what makes it worse."

Sera looked at the dock boards beneath their feet.

"So it's not just the wind."

"No," he said. "It's the water that doesn't leave when it's supposed to."

She glanced toward the house.

Her father's tide log waited on the table inside like proof of that fact.

Beckett stepped back from the edge of the dock and looked toward the horizon.

The clouds had thickened into a low ceiling, the light flattening across the sound until everything looked the same shade of gray.

"Gale watch," he said quietly.

Sera didn't ask how he knew.

She only nodded.

"Do we need plywood?" she asked.

"Not for the house," Beckett said. "But we'll run to town. Get extra straps. Maybe another set of dock screws."

Sera followed him off the dock.

As they stepped back onto the sand, a gust hit hard enough to make the yard gate rattle against its latch.

The sound behind the fence surged higher against the reeds.

Not storm yet.

But the weather had begun turning.

They drove into town just after noon.

The wind had strengthened enough that the truck rocked slightly when they crossed the open stretch near the marsh. The sound no longer lay flat beneath the sky; it moved in restless, overlapping lines, each gust pushing the surface farther into the reeds.

Sera watched the water through the passenger window.

"It's already higher," she said.

"Wind's pushing it in."

"And it stays there."

"For a while."

She nodded.

The road carried more trucks than usual. A small trailer loaded with plywood passed them going the opposite direction.

At the gas station near the hardware store, two men stood beside a boat on a trailer tightening straps across its hull.

No one looked panicked.

Just busy.

Inside the hardware store, the air smelled of damp coats and fresh lumber.

Carla looked up when the door closed behind them.

"Afternoon," she said.

"Afternoon," Beckett replied.

She glanced at the rope and hardware in his hands before he even set them down.

"You tying things down already?" she asked.

"Starting."

She nodded toward the window.

"They're saying gale watch now."

Beckett didn't react.

Sera stepped closer to the counter.

"How long?" she asked.

Carla shrugged.

"Couple days maybe. Nor'easters don't rush."

Beckett placed a small box of dock screws beside the rope.

"That all?" Carla asked.

"For now."

She rang the items up slowly.

Outside, the wind rattled the store's front sign once before settling again.

Carla slid the receipt across the counter.

"Better early than late," she said.

Beckett nodded.

"That's the idea."

Sera thanked her and followed Beckett back out into the wind.

The air had grown noticeably colder while they were inside.

A fine mist had begun drifting across the road—too light to call rain, but steady enough to blur the far edge of the marsh.

They drove home without speaking much.

The truck heater hummed quietly between them.

Sera watched the water again.

The tide should have been falling by now according to the chart on the kitchen table.

But it wasn't.

The wind held it where it was.

When they turned into the yard, Beckett slowed.

Ray's truck sat near the fence.

Ray himself stood near the dock, looking out across the sound with his hands tucked into his jacket.

Beckett parked beside the shed.

Ray glanced over as they stepped out.

"You seeing it?" he said.

Beckett walked toward the dock.

"Yeah."

Ray nodded toward the waterline.

"Already running higher than it should."

Sera followed them down the dock.

The boards creaked under the stronger wind.

Ray tapped one of the pilings with his boot.

"Water stays up long enough," he said, "these'll take the pressure."

Beckett crouched and examined the cleat he had tightened earlier.

Still solid.

But the rope line had already stretched slightly.

Ray looked back toward the house.

"You bring everything in yet?" he asked.

"Most."

"Bring the rest tonight," Ray said. "Wind'll climb after dark."

Sera studied his face.

"You've seen this before," she said.

Ray gave a small smile.

"Few times."

Beckett stood again.

"You worried?"

Ray shook his head once.

"No."

He looked across the sound again, watching the ripples push harder against the reeds.

"Just respectful."

The word hung in the wind between them.

Respect.

Not fear.

Not confidence.

Something quieter.

Ray stepped back from the dock.

"I'll head out," he said. "Got a few things to tie down myself."

Beckett nodded.

"Thanks for the heads up."

Ray lifted his hand once and walked back toward his truck.

The engine started and rolled away down the road.

The yard felt different once he left.

Quieter.

More exposed.

Sera stood beside Beckett at the edge of the dock.

The wind moved steadily across the sound now, pushing the water against the marsh grass so it stayed there rather than slipping back.

"It's holding," she said.

"Yeah."

"That's what you meant earlier."

He nodded.

"The water doesn't leave."

They walked back toward the bay together.

The mist had thickened slightly, tiny droplets catching in Sera's hair as the wind carried them across the yard.

Beckett lifted the bay door the rest of the way down and secured the latch.

Inside, the skiff sat dry and protected.

The repaired seam held clean beneath the dim light.

Sera ran her hand along it once more.

"Still holding," she said.

Beckett watched her hand move across the wood.

"Good work," he replied.

She glanced toward the open side window of the bay.

The wind pressed faintly against the glass.

"You think it'll be bad tonight?" she asked.

"Not tonight."

"Tomorrow?"

"Probably."

She nodded.

The yard had grown darker even though it was still afternoon.

The clouds thickened above the sound until the horizon blurred into the same shade of gray.

Sera stepped outside again and looked toward the marsh.

The waterline had crept farther into the grass.

Only slightly.

But enough to notice.

Behind her, Beckett moved through the bay securing the last loose tools.

The sound of metal latches clicking shut echoed softly in the wind.

By the time he finished, the mist had turned to a thin rain.

Nothing dramatic.

Just the first steady drops.

Beckett stepped onto the porch beside her.

They watched the water rise another inch along the reeds.

"It's starting," Sera said.

He nodded.

"Yeah."

The nor'easter had not arrived yet.

But the island already knew it was coming.

The wind had begun to turn.

And on Hatteras Island, storms rarely arrive alone.

Winter is coming to the island.

Work slows.

Water rises.

And the things the tide uncovers are not always meant to stay buried.

Continue the Story

The journey of Beckett Crowe and Sera Bennett continues in

WHAT THE TIDE KEEPS

Book Two of the Hatteras Island Series

Available now on Amazon.

Readers of *What the Island Asks* often continue directly into Book Two.

About the author

Dr. Joel Cox, writing under the pseudonym **J. Martin**, is a distinguished social scientist whose analytical mind finds its creative counterpart in the world of literary romance. He crafts heartfelt stories that explore the depths of human connection, emotion, and resilience, drawing readers into tender yet profound love stories.

A longtime resident of **Coastal Virginia** and the **North Carolina Outer Banks**, Joel now calls this stunning coastal paradise home, sharing his life full-time with his wife, Lisa. The barrier islands' wild beauty, shifting dunes, and timeless rhythms deeply inspire his writing. When not at his desk, he embraces the active outdoor lifestyle the region offers—casting lines while fishing the inlets, shaping wood in his workshop, grilling fresh catches under open skies, gliding through marshes by kayak, pounding the pavement or trails on runs and bike rides, and immersing himself in the rich language, folklore, and culture that have shaped the Outer Banks for generations.

Though his professional life is grounded in the rigorous study of society and behavior, Joel turns to literary romance as his passionate creative outlet—a space to celebrate love's quiet triumphs, its vulnerabilities, and its enduring power against the backdrop of life's complexities.

This is his debut novel in the genre, a story born from the same thoughtful observation and emotional depth that define both his scholarly work and his life by the sea.

Also by J. Martin